PARADISE CARIBBEAN STYLE

By Melisant Scott

PARADISE CARIBBEAN STYLE

Original © October 26, 2011 Melisant Scott; reprinted ©
April 2, 2012 applies to revision and new cover.
OPEN WINDOW PUBLICATIONS, Texas, USA.
888.204.4144

This book is available in paperback at Open Window
Publications

http://openwindowpublications.com

(ISBN: 0615558593/ISBN-13: 978-0615558592).

Paradise Caribbean Style

DEDICATION

I dedicate this book to my husband, who has been supportive and an inspiration in my efforts of writing. His encouragement helped me to write this contemporary romance about a runaway bride, who literally collides with her male counterpart, sparks ignite and love blossoms.

Introduction

Tiring of the glitter and lights of Hollywood, movie star, heart-throb, Grant Michaels leaves for a much needed holiday to St. Raphael, a small island in the British West Indies. Ill-tempered and frustrated, he seeks solitude and escape. Perchance he meets New York designer, Margaret Stewart and it's love at first sight. Grant meets his female counterpart in Margaret. She's equally successful with men as, he was with women. In fact she on the lam! The animal magnetism between them is no less than sizzling!

Grant has to return to Hollywood unexpectedly when *Tirage Studios* decides to screen female co-stars for his next picture. Disquieted, Grant returns to Hollywood to find he cannot forget the beautiful blonde with the violet eyes. He's disturbed by the undeniable chemistry between them. When he returns to the small island fate reunites them. A summer romance was a complication Margaret never considered, but Grant has other ideas. When Grant discovers Margaret's engaged, he attempts to confront the two-timing blonde only to find she's returned to New York.

Margaret can't believe it when Grant hires her to redecorate his Bel-Air mansion. At first she resists, then it occurs to Margaret, the project could bring notoriety to her design business. Grant's frustrated when Margaret resists his charms. Instead of turning tail and running, women ordinarily flock to him. Seemingly, Margaret Stewart goes out of her way to be difficult.

Grant's never felt about any woman, the way he does with Margaret. When Grant escorts Margaret to his parent's anniversary party, members of his family are determined to play matchmaker. She instantly wins everyone over with her wit and charm. Grant's amazed by his growing interest in her. Just the thought of commitment fills Margaret with trepidation. Especially when it's a man like Grant, who could easily break her heart. Who will be the first to take the plunge when two equally strong personalities meet head on? When sparks ignite and love blossoms, is it possible for two like personalities to come to grips with commitment and find true love?

~****~

Paradise Caribbean Style

Melisant Scott

ACKNOWLEDGMENTS

My special thanks to the many book publishers of the romance genre such as Harlequin Romance, Avon Books, Mira, and Random House, to name a few, which have provided hours of delightful entertainment reading of contemporary romance which is my favorite, my husband, family and my delightful cats who love me no matter what, I wish to extend my gratitude.

Melisant Scott

**Chapter 1**

How could she allow herself to be in this predicament? Margaret Stewart asked herself over and over. This doubt had disturbed her for several days. Particularly now, the wedding was no longer in the planning stages but a reality.

Margaret ignored her instincts considering the sense of doom impaling her as a sign of cold feet. She had faith in her mother's judgment she reminded herself – until now! Trepidation filled Margaret as she stood at the altar with Phillip Lindsay, mentally grasping each word of their marriage vows.

"If anyone objects to this union, speak now or forever hold your piece," the preacher said, pausing for a moment.

Forever was a long time! Margaret considered.

Abruptly she lost control. Hitching her wedding gown to her knees, she forcibly blew a puff of air to remove the veil covering her face. As it billowed forward, she quickly pushed it aside. Margaret gave Phillip a measured look as a wave of self deprecation washed over her. He deserved better. She groaned her displeasure before

leaning to kiss his cheek lightly, she gathered her skirt to her knees and ran down the long aisle toward the front door and out of the church.

In the background she could hear Phillip calling after her, but she never looked back. Instead Margaret flagged down the first cabbie she saw. Her heart was in her throat as she flung the door open and hurried inside. She had never acted so irresponsibly; so rash.

The cab driver gave a quizzical look at her unusual attire and the fact she stood outside a church. Others trailed closely behind. She climbed inside and the cab pulled into traffic. "Where to lady?"

Her mind raced. What to do? Then Margaret remembered she kept a change of clothes in her office in case of an emergency! And this was definitely an emergency! The trip to the office seemed to take hours. At long last she arrived outside the towering skyscraper. Margaret wondered why she stashed thirty dollars inside her garter this morning – now she knew! She paid the cabbie, flung the door open and rushed out.

This was madness she told herself as she rode the elevator to the tenth floor office. She would telephone aunt Kay before she changed her mind. She needed a quiet place. The island of St. Raphael's would distance her from the situation and allow her time to think.

She collected her checkbook and left a note for her family and poor Phillip. The shocked expression on his face she would never forget. It had almost teetered her resolve. Later he would thank her, Margaret thought. She simply realized she could not marry him. Tears streaking her face, she lifted the receiver and punched out her aunt's number. She heaved a deep sigh when Kay Clark answered on the fifth ring. The way things were faring she suspected Kay would not answer at all.

Her voice was a mere squeak. "Aunt Kay?"

"Is that you, Margaret?" Kay asked incredulously.

She paused a moment gathering her thoughts. "Kay, I need a favor." Margaret waited for a response.

Kay realized something was amiss. It was uncharacteristic of her niece to call unexpectedly in a desperate tone of voice. "What's wrong, Margaret?"

"I have to getaway for awhile. Somewhere quiet."

Kay began to worry. "You're always welcome here. But, what's wrong?"

"I'll tell you all about it when I arrive."

~* * * *~

Smoke filled the air with a mixture of jazz and loud conversation in the night club, *Maggie's* on the island of St. Raphael, British West Indies. The club was filled to capacity tonight with a long line extending outside. The moonlight reflected off the Caribbean Sea, as the waves moved endlessly inward to embrace the iridescent white beach of the island cove. The attire was casual and *Maggie's* catered to the upper echelon. The atmosphere was friendly with most people complacent during their wait. There was no competition on the island – *Maggie's* held a monopoly.

Several varieties of tropical plants and a large water fountain were surrounded by wooden tables. The candlelight on each table appeared as fireflies in the darkness. Outside, the music lightly kissed a gentle breeze. Sailboats of various sizes were anchored within view at the marina next door.

After dropping anchor and securing the large sailboat, the *Westwind*, Grant jumped onto the deck. He ambled toward *Maggie's* undecided whether to venture the crowd or simply call it a night. The jazz beckoned him as he ran his hand carelessly through the ebony curls that fell to his brows. The dark eyes were both curious and skeptical. The day was long and the flight from California to St. Raphael in the Leeward Islands exhausted him. He badly needed a vacation Grant thought.

A blissful night's sleep would ease the weariness and mental fatigue he felt. The lack of privacy in his life overwhelmed him at times. He had to escape. Until he found time to consider a solution, Grant suspected the impasse and lack of fulfillment wouldn't leave him. In the past the bright lights and adoring females were enough.

As the line Grant was in moved forward, a young woman greeted him. Smiling, he ordered a scotch and water. After she took his order, the waitress turned to leave. She failed to recognize him, he thought as the young woman departed. Perhaps the moustache and black executive glasses he wore would allow him the privacy he yearned.

Grant sipped his drink and glanced at his watch – eight thirty. Although far from quiet, the place was peaceful he thought. He left California without a word to anyone. Grant recalled the brief telephone conversation with Bill at the airport.

"I need to getaway for awhile," Grant explained. "Take care of things, while I'm away."

"Where are you going?"

"That's not important."

"You can't leave before the picture's completed," Bill pointed out. When no response followed a brief pause, he spoke. "What's with you Grant?" He disliked Grant's moodiness. When life became stressful, Grant simply disappeared. The problem was Grant had no personal life of his own. Bill considered Grant forfeited the right when he decided to become an actor.

"The walls are closing in," Grant said absently.

Bill's wariness was reflected in his voice. "Are we both on the same channel?"

"I don't need a mother," Grant replied impatiently.

Bill groaned his displeasure. For the past three or four months, Grant had been ill-tempered. "You've changed." He paused, waiting for a response. Grant released a haughty sound over the wire. "I'm serious. You better get your act together or you career will be past tense," Bill warned. "I'd like to help. What's eating you?"

He carefully considered Bill's response.

"You're Grant Michaels. The hottest thing with women since Clark Gable and Elvis Presley." Grant gave a low snort of disgust. "*Tirage Studios* won't be happy about this," Bill argued.

"Too bad."

"Your career has flourished for ten years," Bill reminded him. "Take a vacation and come back. This is where you belong," he urged. "Don't throw it away."

"I'll think it over."

And he had since he left Hollywood.

"Sir your table is ready," the young woman said effectively jerking Grant from his reverie. He blinked.

Grant uncoiled his six-foot-five frame from the chair along the water's edge and followed the hostess. Extraordinarily handsome with an irascible smile Grant moved with an air of confidence through the restaurant.

The night club was as he had envisioned with tropical plants, a plush green carpet, bamboo tables and chairs. Ceiling fans circled overhead and antiques were displayed on nearby shelves. The tables encircled a small stage with a piano bar. Nearby a trumpet and saxophone rested. The small combo were on break.

"Welcome to *Maggie's*, I hope you enjoy your meal," the hostess remarked. Flashing a charismatic smile, Grant seated himself. He saw a bewildered expression cross her face as though attempting to place a familiar face. Grant was accustomed to curious lookers and the lack of privacy that followed him.

Moments later the band returned and jazz resonated the club. Grant ordered another scotch and water and started for the men's room. The moment he turned a large planter, he collided with a solid object. Reflexively he snaked his arms out. Embarrassment and surprise gleamed in the violet eyes engaging his. She was as fragrant as a spring day, her skin flawless and soft he discovered.

Mesmerized Grant felt the softness of the silky blonde hair cascading to her waist as their gaze locked for an endless moment. He noticed her eyes sparkled with amusement. Oblivious, he continued to hold her close longer than necessary.

"I'm so sorry," she apologized after an extended moment.

Bewitched with her proximity and beauty, he barely caught her words. "Of course," Grant managed regaining his voice. "Are you alright?"

"I'm fine. Thank you," she replied as he observed the heart shaped lips in graceful movement. "And you?"

Her lips begged to be kissed Grant considered.

She appeared uncomfortable when no response followed and moved to be free of his arms. Reluctantly he lowered them to his sides.

"Excuse me," she said softly, a flirtatious smile curving her lips. After pausing a moment, she moved aside and continued out of the club, looking over her shoulder.

A sense of disappointment swept Grant as he returned to his table. She was the most beautiful creature he had ever seen and he didn't even know her name. He pondered this over the red snapper. The meal however was tasteless to him. Grant dropped a sizeable tip on the table and left the club wondering if he would ever see her again.

The air was cool and the night, clear. He strolled along the water's edge to the beach house he leased for the summer. He would sleep well tonight he thought.

~****~

The following day Grant woke early afternoon in disbelief of how exhausted he was. He stepped into his jeans, combed a hand through his tousled hair and moved downstairs. There was nothing better than a first cup of coffee in the morning, unless he woke with a woman in his arms. A breeze and the sound of the ocean surf greeted him as he opened the patio doors. Sighing Grant brought the cup to his lips.

Miles Davis' tape, *Nefertiti* playing on the stereo, lulled his sensibilities. The sun's radiance brightly reflected off the aquamarine water. What a picturesque scene he thought one couldn't have it closer to heaven than this.

He would telephone his friend, Bill Wallace to explain. Seemingly Bill understood Grant's restlessness, they formed close ties during college. Surely Bill would understand the problem. Grant had reached a crossroads in his life. There were serious decisions to be made that would effect the rest of his life.

Grant's reflective was that Nina prompted this sudden getaway. Each day she conspired to pressure him into a commitment he had no desire to make. True, a thirty-five year old man should concern himself with marriage and a family. But until he felt the way his father did about his mother, Grant preferred to wait.

Grant's thoughts shifted to the blonde goddess he literally collided with the night before. Her violet eyes bewitched him. Given this, his scrambled emotions were soon forgotten. He had to see her again!

~****~

Staring at the ceiling, Margaret recalled the humiliation. She could live a thousand years and never encounter anyone with more hands. Why had she agreed to meet Harold Wilson? It was because of aunt Kay's persistence, a tiny voice supplied.

Margaret regretted the manner in which she fled the restaurant, almost knocking over a tall, handsome stranger. Vividly she recalled those piercing dark eyes. They possessed the power to penetrate to her soul. She had never experienced anything like it, and this disturbed Margaret. Who was he?

From the moment they collided, she was inexplicably drawn to him. He was handsome of to say the least but that wasn't it. Margaret hadn't let matters of this nature trouble her in the past. She could have her choice of most men. Her innate charm kept the male gender coming back. But the stranger's arms about her felt so right.

Margaret shook herself mentally. She would bask in the sun and take advantage of the leisure time she thought. Aunt Kay was gracious to accept her under the circumstances. It seemed she had taken running away to her repertoire. She had worked hard at building a clientele for her business, *Unicorn Designs*. And now with the added pressure of marriage it had been too much for her she reasoned. She realized when she went into business it would not be easy and it hadn't been. She earned everything by working hard and by her sheer persistence. Her degrees in design and marketing served her well. Margaret was excellent in the social graces, born with brains and beauty that intimidated most men. Men were never a problem for Margaret if anything it came too easily.

"Good morning, Margaret," Kay greeted as her niece engaged the last step of the stairwell.

She kissed her aunt Kay's cheek. "Did you sleep well, dear?"

Smiling, Kay said, "Yes, I did. Would you care for some coffee?"

Margaret nodded as she took a seat at the table. It wasn't long before Margaret mentioned her date the night before. Kay was aghast that a quiet man like Harold Wilson could behave distastefully in public. Much later, the women reminisced of old times.

Finally Margaret ventured to ask. "Do you know a tall, dark man with a moustache and glasses?" she queried.

Kay considered the question before answering. She shook her head and said, "Not that I recall. Should I?"

Margaret answered in tone she hoped was one of mild curiosity. "Last night on the way out of the restaurant, I almost knocked him over," Margaret confessed. "I was so embarrassed."

"You ran out of the restaurant?" Kay asked incredulously. "I don't believe it."

"When Harold's hand moved up my thigh," Margaret's voice trailed off. Kay gave a disgusted sound. Margaret raised both hands in a helpless gesture.

"Just wait until, I get my hands on him," Kay replied, agitation evident in her eyes. "He will regret his lewd behavior."

Margaret heaved a deep sigh. Once Kay warmed to a subject she could be tenacious. Margaret thought she should focus Kay's attentions elsewhere.

"Why did you name the club, *Maggie's*?"

For a moment Kay stared back in disbelief. She recognized the determined expression on her niece's face. Margaret wasn't prepared to discuss what brought her to the island. "It seemed appropriate and might I add, after three years in business, *Maggie's* doing well," Kay remarked proudly as she folded her arms along her paunchy waistline.

Margaret's mind raced as aunt Kay continued her tirade. She caught little of the conversation; her thoughts were a million miles away.

Kay's animated face was kind. Margaret remembered Kay married a man employed by a large electronics corporation. Five years ago Jim Clark, her husband of thirty years died leaving Kay sizeable investments and a large insurance policy.

Margaret lost contact with Kay after Jim's death. According to Kay, she wandered aimlessly for two years then opened a restaurant and bar on the island. Voile, the birth of *Maggie's*. Kay maintained contact with Margaret's mother, Elisia Stewart. The sisters differed as night from day, although a true love bonded them. Elisia a true yuppie, raised her only daughter with all the refinements, and Margaret grew up surrounded by love. Since Kay and Jim were childless she focused her motherly instincts on her niece.

Pleasantly surprised Margaret recalled the handsome stranger's face. She was drawn to him from the beginning. This was unfamiliar turf for Margaret. She didn't have a clue to her continued thoughts of the brief encounter. Who was he?

~****~

**Chapter 2**

"Bachy, stop! Leave the man alone," she exclaimed.

Was he dreaming? The beautiful woman he met last night was approaching him – wet, round and glistening. What's the awful noise? Grant wondered. He lurched forward as Margaret leaned down to lift Bachy in her arms. The movement brought their lips inches apart. The terrier took leave when he saw the leash in her hand. A sharp gasp escaped her parted lips as the fabric of her suit strained in an attempt to cover her breasts.

Instinctively Grant's arm encircled her neck, pulling her into his lap. He'd wanted to kiss her senseless last night, but the temptation now was more than any man could resist. She held herself rigid at first, and slowly her posture relaxed as Grant massaged her spine. She tasted much better than he'd fantasized. His arms tightened around her waist as her bosom brushed the sensitive hairs of his chest. Of its own volition his tongue probed and gained entry to spar with hers in the ageless primal ritual. Grant deepened the kiss as he experienced an ache in his loins.

Bachy growled effectively bringing Margaret to her senses, she withdrew. Appalled by the liberties he'd easily taken, she swung her hand to contact his face.

"How dare you!" she squealed with indignation. Her eyes mirrored her anger.

"You shouldn't make it a practice to throw yourself at a man," Grant growled. Instantly he took her wrist in a vice grip before her withdrawal. She tried to slap him with her free hand but he captured it effortlessly in mid air. A smirk on his face, he pushed to his feet and drew her to his chest.

Margaret was set aback by his reaction. The dark eyes became shuttered. Grasping her hand in one large masculine hand, Grant slanted his mouth over hers. This time the kiss lacked passion, it was punishing. He traced the recess behind her ear with his tongue and kissed the hollow of her neck. Margaret's nipples hardened as his powerful thighs brushed firmly against hers. Abruptly as it began, Grant set her from him. Unaccustomed to this treatment from any man, she was perplexed.

"You animal!" she yelled to his retreating figure. He responded with a low rich laugh. Angry she moved her fingers to her lips in remembrance. Her lower lip was swollen from the assault. She struggled to hold onto her ill-temper. Just the same she began to feel warm, feminine and desirable.

In the past Margaret had always called the shots with the men in her life. In any event this was unfamiliar turf to her. Whereas several men had proposed marriage, she never heard bells nor experienced butterflies when they kissed her. Not the same as the handsome stranger made her feel she'd never experienced anything like this. Margaret was pleased. She wondered at one point if she had the capacity for love. Her innate ability to attract the male gender came easily for Margaret. She reasoned this accounted for her lack of involvement on an emotional level, it took the challenge out of the experience.

The tall stranger wreaked with virility. Margaret suspected an attraction of this magnitude tipped the Richter scales past eight. Margaret bathed as she recalled the afternoon at the beach. Her thoughts centered on the stranger, he bewitched her. Who was he? Margaret wondered moving a hand to her chin. Her lips tingled with anticipation of a reunion. She would learn his name.

Smiling Kay entered the house with a bag of groceries in each arm. She deposited the bags with a plop on the countertop. Moving into the kitchen she issued instructions to the housekeeper for the evening meal.

Margaret could not disguise her curiosity. "What's this about aunt Kay?"

"I've planned a small dinner party tonight, just a few friends." Kay patted Margaret's shoulder in a motherly fashion. "Wear something pretty."

~****~

Pleased with her reflection, Margaret's eyes scanned the French plait at her nape, the topaz lounging pantsuit and silver earrings she wore.

Tonight twelve guests were expected for the dinner party. Was this aunt Kay's idea of a small party? Margaret wondered preening herself in the hallway mirror. When she turned, her eyes riveted on a beautiful Latin woman alongside the tall handsome stranger. She learned his name was Grant Michaels. The last guest was an attractive man, Peter Constanza. Kay lingered in her introduction of Peter. He was dashing with broad shoulders and the gleam in Peter's eyes indicated he liked what he saw.

Everyone enjoyed conversation over drinks in the living room. Had it been her imagination? Margaret thought a smirk covered Grant's face as they were introduced.

The man was incorrigible!

The Latin beauty was Tonya Rivera. Her wavy brunette hair framed her almond eyes. Margaret had to admit her figure was flawless. She noticed that Tonya clung possessively to Grant's arm. It was clear she considered him her property.

Why had Grant behaved in the manner he had today on the beach when he was evidently involved with Tonya? Not that Margaret blamed him in the least of being attracted to the Latin beauty.

As the evening passed the stereo played a collage of relaxing music and Margaret felt restive. She managed to outmaneuver Peter's clever ministrations. His persistence disturbed her.

"At last we meet," Peter said gazing into her eyes. After much effort he managed to corner Margaret. "Your aunt speaks fondly of you and after our meeting, I can see why. You're lovely, Margaret Stewart."

Margaret smiled gracefully although it was far from what she felt at the moment. Occasionally she would dart her eyes in Grant's direction. The man must have radar she considered. He was always aware of her eyes on him. When their eyes met Grant would nod his head subtlety.

The sounds of the party faded as Grant's thoughts moved the events earlier in the day. "Damn!" Grant exclaimed hopping on one foot, after stumping his toe. The telephone continued to ring insistently. "Yes? Hello?"

"Grant?" A voice greeted him over the wire.

"I almost killed myself trying to reach the phone. "What's wrong, Bill?"

"Well I don't want to alarm you, however I have things to discuss with you. First the good news, your parents would like to hear from you. Second, Artie called and has scripts he wants you to consider for your next film. Nina has called night and day trying to locate you. Please get the woman off my back! Now the bad news you'll have to fly back for one week," Bill answered.

"Why? And it had better be good!"

"It seems the director at *Tirage Studios* requires your illustrious presence to help them choose your co-star for the new film in September. He wants you to rehearse with the women they're considering for the part, costumes, and so forth."

"That can wait. I've only arrived.

"Apparently not, Artie tells me everyone is upset because they've been unable to reach you," Bill said, "Sorry pal. A week's not forever."

"Damn! When?"

"Immediately."

"I'll fly out tomorrow. But only for a week!"

It was always this way whenever he tried to getaway. Damn it anyway! Grant poured himself a cognac. They would not leave him alone for a minute. He telephoned Artie and arranged a meeting for Tuesday. Afterward he dialed his parents number in San Diego.

"Mom? It's Grant."

"Where are you? Are you alright? I've been sick with worry!" Judith Michaels exclaimed.

"Mom, calm down. I'm fine. I forgot to call," he confessed. "Listen, I'm flying in tomorrow. Do you think dad could pick me up at the airport?"

"Of course. Now where are you?"

"I'm on a small island in the British West Indies."

"What was your rationale for going there?"

"I'll tell you about it tomorrow. Tell dad I'll be on flight 49 arriving at two in the afternoon on Crown Airlines," Grant said with a smile reflected in his voice. After a few moments Grant jerked himself back to the present and moved to join the others at the dining table.

Peter settled himself next to Margaret at the dinner table. He talked incessantly of himself and his business throughout the meal. Beneath her outward smile, Margaret was bored and peeved.

When Tonya laughed the hair on Margaret's nape stood on end. She couldn't bear watching the Latin temptress whisper in Grant's ear. Why would this disturb her? Margaret wondered because he hadn't made a play for her attentions.

Soft jazz resonated throughout the house to create a relaxing atmosphere. Someone opened the French doors leading onto a garden patio. Some of the group ambled outside to enjoy the splendid view. Seth and Kay moved in rhythm to the slow jazzy tune. Grant and Tonya danced provocatively. Everyone seemed to enjoy themselves, except Margaret.

Peter observed Tonya appreciatively as she danced with Grant. When Margaret glanced upward, Peter and Tonya were dancing thigh to thigh. A shadow fell across Margaret's chair as she turned. Towering over her was Grant, his hand extended to her. His eyes held hers for an extended moment. Margaret's heart fluttered in her throat.

"Dance with me," Grant said more a statement than a request.

Smiling under lowered lashes, Margaret accepted his hand. His movements were fluid as he guided her to the tune. Margaret loved the musk scent her wore. When the song ended and another began, she attempted to pull back, Grant gathered her close as he nuzzled his face into her hair.

He whispered, "Are you afraid?"

She countered, "Did you forget about Tonya?"

Grant drew her closer than necessary. "She's with Peter."

Before she realized what was happening, he drew her from the crowd indicating they should leave the party.

Along the Caribbean beach line, Margaret stooped to slip out of her sandals. Following her lead, Grant removed his shoes.

"They'll never miss us," he coaxed extending his hand to her.

"What makes you so sure of yourself?" Margaret asked with a cheeky grin. Grant shot her a knowing smile.

Neither spoke for several moments as they walked along the water's edge. It was as if both sensed the mutual need to be alone. The moon's bright reflection off the water created a romantic atmosphere. Grant halted, pivoted toward Margaret, and cupped her chin tenderly in one hand. Gazing into the violet pools, he lowered his head. Grant's lips lightly brushed hers – testing, teasing. His tongue traced her lower lip.

He moved her hand to his lips, kissing each fingertip. This sent pulsing waves throughout her nervous system. His hands moved to her thighs as he drew her firmly against him.

"Margaret …" he repeated through ragged breaths.

She couldn't remember how they wound up on the sand. He unbuttoned her blouse and exposing her breasts in their lacy confines. A thumb slipped inside to massage a rosy bud as he nuzzled the other with his cheek.

"Grant, stop," she whimpered.

He unfastened her brassiere as he pressed his length against hers. Margaret could feel his heartbeat echo her own. He took a rosy peak in his mouth, tasting and suckling until she moaned and arched toward him.

"Margaret, you don't know what you do to me."

"Kiss me," she encouraged.

He pushed up on one elbow. Margaret failed to understand his withdrawal.

"I'm sorry," he choked out as his breathing began to slow. Margaret sensed his restraint was barely subdued as violet eyes gazed deeply into smoky brown.

Pushing to a seated position, Grant tucked his shirt into his pants as he inhaled and exhaled audibly. Confused and frustrated, Margaret pulled her blouse together. The ease in which he accomplished the seduction irked her. She trembled with the thought if he hadn't stopped.

Margaret mused, was he was a warlock?

"Something wrong?" Margaret asked softly.

"You're a desirable woman," Grant said quietly, his back to her.

"What happened?"

"There's a powerful chemistry between us. I know you feel it, too." Grant gave her an engaging smile. "Even the first time we collided."

Unable to deny the primitive emotions he elicited within her, she nodded. Grant drew Margaret to her feet and gently folded her to him. Closing his eyes, he rested his chin against the top of her head, as a sigh escaped his lips. Margaret could hear the drumbeat of his heart.

"An attraction like ours will not be denied," he said huskily. "I want to spent time with you."

Margaret refused to admit he frightened her. She adopted what she hoped was a casual tone. "Our hormones are in control at the moment."

His eyes searched hers for several moments, his brows coming together in a frown. No further words were spoken, as they walked with arms linked to the beach house.

As the two approached the patio, Kay said casually, "It's a lovely night for a walk."

Unaware of their disheveled appearance, Grant and Margaret exchanged an anxious look.

"Aunt Kay it was a wonderful party," Margaret replied, surprised at the control in her voice. "Where's Peter? I would like to say goodnight."

Kay cleared her throat. "When he and Tonya couldn't find the two of you, they left together."

Margaret uttered an embarrassed sound more to herself.

Yawning, Kay moved a hand to her mouth as she turned to leave. "I'm exhausted. Goodnight," she said moving into the house.

Grant turned to Margaret as both broke into spontaneous laughter.

"I have to leave tomorrow for Hollywood," Grant began. Margaret's smile turned to a frown. He continued, "There's no choice in the matter. I'll be gone for a week. How long is your stay?"

"I'll be here awhile longer." She paused to listen.

"What I was about to say is, go sailing with me when I return? I want to give us time to become acquainted with one another." His eyes pleaded with hers, he took her hand in his.

Margaret shook her head. "I'm not going to have an affair with you. Maybe this is for the best?" Frankly she did not believe her own words. Fear motivated her.

"I wouldn't let things get out of hand," Grant said on a lighter note. His boyish look of sincerity was reflected as his brows lifted in question.

"Grant, my life is complicated as it is." His eyes implored hers. "I'll think it over," Margaret said smiling.

~****~

**Chapter 3**

Even though Grant had been in California for three days, he lifted the telephone receiver several times to call Margaret, only to cradle it. No doubt she considered a relationship between them impossible.

"Grant?"

He shook his head to clear the muddle. "What?"

"Break! Take fifteen minutes and try to remember what we're doing here, please!" the director admonished.

Grant had trouble focusing on his work. In his mind's eye, Margaret … their naked, wet bodies moved as one in a natural rhythm. After he was fitted by wardrobe, Grant scanned several scripts with Artie and ended the day with dinner at his long time friend and manager's home, Bill Wallace.

Difficult though it was, Grant attempted to make small talk. "How are you and the little woman?" he asked lifting the glass of iced tea to his lips.

"She wants another baby. Apparently Jeremy's to big to cuddle anymore," Bill said in mock exasperation.

"We should all be so lucky."

"Were you lonely down in the Caribbean, Grant?"

"Not at all."

"What's there to do besides snorkeling, swimming or sailing? I'm sure it's all relaxing, but don't you miss the women?" Bill inquired jokingly as he brought his hands to his chest imitating a woman with a large bust. "And getting laid?"

"Well, I did meet this one woman."

"Women were never a problem for you. Is she good?"

"It's not like that," Grant interrupted. "Margaret's different. She's a beautiful blonde, intelligent, sensitive and passionate."

"Oh come now, what about Nina? Spare me the hearts and flowers. She must have great ..." Again Bill brought his hands to cup his chest.

His anger escalated. Bill rose from the chair.

"As soon as you've bedded her, she'll be like the rest – history." Bill chuckled.

Grant stood in one swift movement and swung his fist contacting Bill's jaw.

"What's got into you," Bill growled rubbing his chin. "Are you crazy?"

"I won't have you talk about Margaret that way!" Grant shouted. Presently he regretted his impulsive behavior. He heaved a deep sigh. "I'm sorry."

"You're serious," Bill responded in amazement. "I don't believe it. You're in love."

"I enjoy her company."

"I'd like to meet this Margaret. She must be something if she has managed to corral you – the Hollywood playboy!"

"Perhaps you will," Grant replied.

In love? What a laugh, Grant considered.

~****~

Nina Albright will be your next co-star. We'll increase the public's interest in the two of you as a couple," Artie explained. "You'll be seen everywhere together."

"That's impossible. I'm leaving in three days," Grant supplied.

Ignoring Grant's response, Artie continued, "I'll call for dinner reservations. Later you'll take her dancing. The newspapers and magazines will love it."

That night Grant and Nina dined in French cuisine and enjoyed the red carpet treatment. It was all superficial he thought. Cameras flashed everywhere. Nina was ravishing with henna hair, large green eyes and her slim figure and small bust.

"Grant, I've missed you. Why did you leave without telling anyone?" Nina whispered in his ear as they moved to the music.

"Something came up unexpectedly," he lied. "I'm sorry."

"You're a bad boy, Grant," Nina scolded. "But I'm prepared to forgive you, should you pop the question."

"We have to talk." Grant nudged her toward the door.

He drove Nina home in the Jaguar the studio rented for the night. Turning the ignition off, Grant began, "Look Nina, I am fond of you. You deserve someone who will love you and want what you've described. I'm not that man. I respect you enough to be honest. This is for publicity. You're a beautiful woman, I'm sure you'll have no trouble."

"You can't blame a girl for trying," Nina said kissing his cheek. "Where will you go?"

"Somewhere quiet and restful for the summer. I'll see you in September."

Nina squeezed his hand. "Goodbye, Grant."

~****~

"I suppose this is goodbye. Stay in touch, your mother worries," Bill said.

"I'll call soon as I reach St. Raphael's," Grant replied.

Both men embraced as the last call for Grant's flight was announced. Waving, Grant boarded the plane.

Seven days passed since Grant's departure. He yearned for the tranquility of St. Raphael's and a certain blonde. He missed seeing the sparkle of amusement in Margaret's eyes when she smiled. Grant hadn't experienced emotions like this for a woman. The entire time he was in California he thought of nothing else.

Approaching St. Raphael's, the amphibian aircraft glided onto the water. Grant unloaded his baggage and bid the pilot farewell. He was here at last!

Nonchalantly Grant walked, his gaze scanned the surroundings as if the first time. Hypnotized by the spectacular view, he stood outside *Maggie's* staring out to sea.

Kay and Margaret stepped back to admire their efforts, the preparations for the small dinner party tonight were compelling. Staying busy hadn't given Margaret time to brood over Grant. She knew his life wasn't his own as an actor, he belonged to the public. Margaret saw a man standing outside the club. Still unable to distinguish who he was, Margaret left the club. As she moved closer to the silhouette, she queried, "Grant?"

He turned, a transfixed expression on his face. "Hello, Margaret," Grant said with a reluctant smile.

With the encounter his eyes briefly mirrored her confusion, Margaret considered. "How are you?" she asked.

"Glad to be here," he said wearily.

"Have you just arrived?"

"A few minutes ago. I'm pleased you noticed my absence."

"Can I buy you a drink? Hungry?" Margaret questioned trying to conceal her delight.

"In answer to both questions, yes."

"We'd be pleased if you'd join our dinner party tonight. Suddenly aunt Kay has become social. I think she's got a crush on Seth, a long time friend. There's a bar. What do you say?"

A smile played on Grant's face. "What an idea, I accept."

She relieved him of one of the small bags he carried, as they started in the direction of his beach house.

"What a view of the ocean. How did you ever find it?" Margaret exclaimed. She sat the bag on the chair.

"The place belongs to a friend of mine. I'll take a shower and change before we go?"

"Here, take this with you," Margaret said offering him a glass of cabernet. "It will help relax you."

Smiling Grant accepted the drink and started for the shower. "Thanks. I'll be out in a few minutes, and we'll leave."

Thirty minutes later, he returned.

"Welcome back," Margaret greeted.

"Where did this all come from?" Grant asked puzzled, pointing to the table.

"While you showered, I called the club and asked them to send over Lasagna Primavera, salad and garlic bread." She motioned for him to take a seat at the table.

Candlelight illuminated the dining area, a lacy beige cloth adorned the table with formal settings. A gentle breeze blew through the patio doors.

"It's great to be here – to enjoy your company," Grant supplied, sipping the cabernet.

"You never did tell me what brought you to the Caribbean?" Margaret ventured with a broad smile.

"My work is demanding," Grant began. "The summer here will help me recharge. How about you?"

A breeze spilled his ebony hair over his brows lending him a rakish look in the navy and white striped tee-shirt and white slacks he wore. Everything about the man was perfection from the handsome chiseled features to his lean sinewy body. A man capable of breaking a woman's heart Margaret considered. Grant smiled as he shifted his gaze in Margaret's direction. Ignoring his question, she questioned, "What is your work?" He didn't appear as someone who worked with their hands, they were much too soft.

She was evading the question Grant considered, he released a low, rich laugh. She was easily made nervous he thought. It appeared each had a knack for catching the other off guard. "I'm a corporate executive for an industrial research firm in California. Vital statistics are: I am thirty-five, the youngest of three children. My parents reside in San Diego, as do my sisters, Anna and Rachael," he answered in a teasing tone.

"Never married?" Margaret couldn't believe the words escaped her.

Slanting her a sidelong look he teased, "Guess I haven't met the right woman. How about you?"

"I was married once. At thirty it's hard to understand what drives one at nineteen," she remarked wistfully.

Grant remained silent but attentive.

"I eloped with a young man my parents detested. He followed a wild crowd. He was exciting compared to the sheltered life I'd led. Six months later he did not come home one day. I learned he was arrested during the robbery of a convenience store. My parents filed a divorce in my behalf."

"You were young," he offered. Grant wasn't sure what to say. Margaret became withdrawn. "How about a drink?"

"Great," she murmured in an attempt to focus her thoughts. Forcing a smile, she nodded. Grant possessed an unusual quality for listening, Margaret thought. She found herself conveying experiences to him she had never related to anyone. What brought on this attack of conscious she mused. She shook herself mentally, focus! "Tell me more about yourself?" she encouraged.

"I've been pampered by my parents and grandparents, and my sisters as well," Grant remarked.

"It's easy to care for someone who is sensitive, unpretentious and sincere," Margaret found herself saying. Where did that come from?

After dinner, they moved onto the patio. Margaret blamed her giddiness on the wine. Several minutes later, she shifted to massage his tense shoulders and neck.

"Uh-h-h …that feels good," he murmured. Closing his eyes, Grant exhaled slowly. "Margaret, that's wonderful." Her lips brushed his neck.

Whimsically he tugged her into his lap. "I warn you, woman. I may forget you're being hospitable." His mirthful eyes changed to darkened pools. Their gazes locked.

"It's been a wonderful day," Margaret said, experiencing a pang of regret it was ending. She considered it best to leave before the situation became unmanageable."

"My pleasure," Grant replied. He recognized this as his cue, the time had ended. "Let's take it slow," he said quietly in response to the unspoken question in her eyes. "I'll see you to the door."

Today Margaret felt a closeness formed between them. Why had his eyes darkened? She couldn't fathom the sudden change. She wondered what it would be like to have his strong arms caress her while they made love. Would he be a gentle or aggressive lover? Margaret yearned to learn more about Grant Michaels. Seemingly he drew her like a magnet, confusing and intriguing her at the same time. He's a complicated man, and Margaret suspected she was in big trouble.

"Yes, of course." She started for the door.

"Margaret?"

She turned to glance over her shoulder. "Yes?"

"Go sailing with me tomorrow?" Grant ventured. "I want to spend time with you."

"Call me tomorrow." She continued out the door. "Goodnight."

~****~

Enveloped in a dreamy haze, Margaret thought she heard someone at the door. The sound persisted. Dressed in satin short pajamas she went to the door. Who would call at this hour? Margaret thought opening the door.

Grant stood in the doorway, pure male satisfaction covered his face as he appraised her.

"Do you make it a habit of answering the door dressed so enticing?" he asked with a suggestive grin.

Margaret was thrown off balance momentarily.

"What brings you here," she asked irritably.

"You agreed to go sailing," Grant pointed out.

He has an answer for everything she considered.

"Come inside," Margaret moved to allow him entry. "I'm not dressed."

"No hurry." Grant's eyes twinkled with amusement as he cornered her against the wall. "Take all the time you need."

Uncomfortable she tried to hide her nakedness, her ample bosom and shapely legs. Margaret ducked under his arm and ran upstairs. "Make yourself at home. I'll be down in a few minutes."

Twenty minutes later, Margaret joined Grant in the living room and they started for the marina. Grant led her over to a forty-foot, sloop called, the *Westwind*. He drew anchor and prepared for launch from the boat slip.

Once they left the marina, the sails caught wind, and Grant discovered a secluded cove miles away. Margaret enjoyed watching Grant handle the large sailboat and explain how much he loved sailing. His handsome chiseled features made her heart palpitate.

He dropped anchor and they climbed from the sailboat and started for the iridescent beach. The tropical flora and fauna were picturesque. The area untouched by man, it was a beautiful tropical garden. They unpacked the supplies for the picnic, slipped out of their shorts, and decided to take in a swim before the picnic.

Grant was a strong swimmer and moved far ahead of Margaret in the warm, emerald waters. The sun against an azure sky was entrancing. Margaret was busy taking the scenery in that she hadn't noticed Grant moved farther ahead in the water. After a thirty minute swim, the two started for the beach line to enjoy their picnic.

Margaret unpacked the picnic basket after spreading a blanket on the sand. "It looks wonderful, Grant. The swim was refreshing and the food looks great. You've gone to a lot of trouble for this. I have to ask, why me?"

"Why would you ask?" Grant shot her a puzzled look as he was drying himself."

"Grant, I like you and today has been wonderful," Margaret began. "But this is a summer vacation for us. We have to remember this and keep it in context."

"What are you afraid of Margaret? That you might enjoy yourself?" Grant gave a broad smile.

"I'm not going to have an affair with you, Grant," Margaret insisted.

Propelled as if by unknown forces, Grant angled his mouth over hers. A fierce heat ignited within him. She stroked his back and combed her fingers through his hair. Blatantly, she traced his lips with her tongue to gain entry. His response was a guttural moan. His hand moved to her breasts.

"Margaret, I want to feel, to taste you," he encouraged.

"You promised-" Margaret's voice lacked conviction.

"I've tried to forget the attraction. I want to make love to you."

"No."

"C'mon, Margaret. The way your body responds, I know you desire me. Don't deny it!"

Submissive to her traitorous body she leaned into Grant and he plundered kisses along her mouth and neck. He stood in one swift movement cradling her knees with his arm, he lifted her.

Her arm enveloped his neck. Sighing she buried her face in his chest.

He moved to an area where they spread a blanket on the sand. Grant set her on her feet as their gaze locked.

"You're beautiful. I want you."

"Kiss me," she whispered.

Without encouragement, he cupped the back of her head as his lips took possession of hers. Margaret pulled his shirt free and began to unbutton it, pushing it feverishly over his shoulders. Her hands caressed the lean, taunt musculature of his abdomen; moreover the dark hair on his chest. Grant inhaled sharply and for a moment, held his breath.

Deliberately, he explored her body with the same deliberate strokes, his hands trailed along her ribs, then settled on her soft breasts. He could feel the erect peaks under her blouse. He lifted the hem of her pullover and removed it.

He couldn't wait to experience the sensation of flesh upon flesh. Releasing her bra, he sent the garment to the floor. A flush of embarrassment covered Margaret. Suddenly she lifted her hands to cover her breasts.

"Please … don't," he requested seductively.

Reluctantly she moved them to her sides. Grant considered her perfection. She was the most beautiful woman he'd ever seen. Just looking at her made him tingle with anticipation. He became hard. It would take all the will power he could muster to keep from rushing her. His body responded to her was as though his being was dependent upon one thing – possessing her.

Take it slow he told himself, attempting to calm the surge of emotions. Lowering himself next to her on the sand, he encouraged her to join him. He kissed her with a fierce tenderness. She was a woman capable of driving a man wild with desire. Grant could lose himself in the violet pools. He wondered how it would be to have her naked beneath him. An insatiable hunger seized him. Grant ground his hips against hers.

"You're like a newly discovered intoxicating sensation, Margaret. Touch me," he rasped between kisses.

Spreading her magic, Margaret massaged his back and hips. She moaned his name several times, her hands urging him onward to the fulfillment she desired. A soft moan escaped her as Grant took her nipple in his mouth, his tongue circled, teasing. Her pulse bounded with excitement. His touch heightened her sensibilities.

He gasped as Margaret's hand swept to the plane of his stomach. Breathing raggedly, he ached for her.

Margaret felt his swelling desire as he shifted. She moved into his embrace. It had to be the fourth of July. She felt as though fireworks had exploded within.

With their garments discarded, he drew her closer. Grant lost control, he took possession of her mouth in a slow deliberate rhythm. This was heaven he considered. They fit together like two integral parts of a puzzle.

Margaret had never experienced such ecstasy. She moved her hands upward along his sides. Passing briefly along his nipples, she traced each with a thumb. He moaned a throaty sound.

"You don't know what you do to me," he managed.

"I have a good idea," she teased. "What do you want?"

"You," he responded, moving closer. Grant could wait no longer. He took her and the volcanic eruptions kissed the heavens, molten and consuming. They rocketed skyward, climbing and swirling together, moving in unison as one.

It was a pleasure beyond description. As though she discovered what she spent her whole life in search. This man was the ultimate lover – gentle, passionate and confident.

Spent they drifted to sleep in one another's arms.

~****~

**Chapter 4**

What was the terrible noise? Grant wondered. The alarm? The ringing continued. Half awake, Grant answered, "Hello?"

"Son?"

Grant shook his head and rubbed his eyes as he focused on the conversation. "Mom, I'm fine. The flight was pleasant." He paused, listening. "Call me later?"

Smiling to herself Margaret sat up in bed. She threw back the covers and swung her legs off.

Grant heard the shower and was determined to resume where they had left off. Accompanying her into the shower, he tenderly pulled her into his arms and kissed her. She was sweet and soft against his hardness. He couldn't get enough of her. What was it about this woman? Similar to his first time, it scared the hell out of him.

As if a physical blow was delivered to her chest, Margaret was breathless. Suddenly she was aware of her deep feelings for this man. Did he experience similar emotions? Searching his eyes, Margaret saw desire and admiration.

"You're beautiful. So soft and sweet …" He did not complete the statement. Once again they made love. This time he wanted to pleasure a woman more than himself.

Outside the shower, Grant dried her with great care. He was sure he stood midst the fallout after an explosion. The explosion had been within himself. She stimulated inexplicable feelings.

"I'll walk you home unless you prefer to stay the night?" he began.

"I'd like that."

"Which?" Grant teased.

"I'd better go."

"I was afraid of that." On a serious note, he began, "Margaret, I've enjoyed," Somehow the words weren't coming out right. "I want to see you again. How long will you stay?"

"Two weeks."

Lightly stroking her cheek with the back of his hand, he whispered, "We have so little time."

"I'm flattered."

"Don't be. I am sincere. We need more time to explore what's happening here."

"If you're certain that's what you want."

Grant's brows came together in an enigmatic expression, he growled as he gripped her shoulders and held her at distance. "I can't remember when I've enjoyed being with a woman more." Margaret stared at him incredulously. "Damn right, I'm sure!"

A short time later they arrived at the Clark residence. He lightly brushed her lips with his, then turned to take his leave. "I'll call you tomorrow."

"Goodnight, Grant."

The night was unforgettable and she was thoroughly confused. Margaret couldn't believe the uncharacteristic change, she was not one to have a casual affair. She reviewed the night's events until sleep claimed her.

The next day she was at peace with the world. Leisurely she prepared for it. The telephone rang.

"Good morning," a voice greeted.

"Hello?" Margaret answered. Silence followed.

"Who's calling, please?" she asked with apprehension.

"Someone eager for your company."

"Grant?"

"Who else?" he laughed.

"How are you?" she inquired.

"I'll be much better once I see you again."

"That's sweet but unnecessary," she remarked curtly.

"What are you saying?" Grant couldn't fathom the tension in her voice.

"Look we had a nice evening. End of story," Margaret ground out.

"Margaret, I want to see you," he said hesitantly in an effort to quell his agitation.

Silence.

"Dammit. Answer me!" His voice succinct, he continued. "Do you want to see me again?"

"Last night does not obligate you," she supplied. She regretted the words escaped her.

"I never do anything that does not please me," he explained as if she were a child. "I don't consider my time with you an obligation."

Margaret was dumbfounded. "I, uh …"

"I'll pick you up in an hour. We'll spend the day at the beach." He rang off.

Grant packed a cooler with drinks and snacks for the afternoon, then started for the Clark home to collect Margaret.

~****~

Snorkeling, Margaret saw several brightly colored fish. The ocean floor was alive with various colors. It was a whole new world below the water's surface she considered. An hour and half later they made for shore.

"Your shoulders are peeling," Grant offered as he came up behind her. He squeezed suntan lotion on his palm and began to rub it on her back.

"How thoughtful," Margaret said, glancing over her shoulder.

"Will you join me for dinner tonight?"

"Grant, we've spent the entire day together," she said dryly.

"Why do you persist in being difficult?" Exasperated he continued, "I thought we could dine at the club and dance."

Tilting her head, Margaret narrowed her eyes. She studied his expression with calm reserve. When he appeared nonplussed, she relented. "Alright."

"I think this is the beginning of a beautiful relationship, swe-e-e-t-heart," Grant said, mocking Bogart.

"You're incorrigible!"

"I cer-tainly hope so," he replied, wriggling his eyebrows like Groucho Marx.

~****~

"You're a sight to behold," Grant murmured approvingly, his eyes perused her.

"Thank you. Please come in," Margaret invited.

Kay entered the room curious about the visitor at the door. "I see you've come courting."

"Aunt Kay!" Margaret admonished.

"It's alright. Yes, I have at that," he chuckled. "Hello, Kay."

"Good evening," Kay greeted. "Be sure to have her home by a decent hour. You hear me, young man?"

"Yes, ma'am," Grant said with a polite nod of his head.

"We're having dinner at the club. Good night, Kay," Margaret said kissing her aunt's cheek. Her eyes brooked no further comment.

Maggie's buzzed with conversation and music. They were shown to a table near the musicians. While they waited for the entrée both enjoyed easy conversation over a drink. Grant was handsome in the dark suit he wore Margaret thought. She marveled how his incandescent eyes sparkled with amusement as he spoke. She noticed his eyes left her momentarily to order.

He chuckled to himself. "What is it?" Margaret asked.

"Forgive me, I was thinking about what your aunt said earlier. I haven't heard anything like it since I was in high school," Grant explained. "She cares for you a great deal."

"Aunt Kay has always been protective."

"Will you miss the island when you return to New York," Grant questioned as he reached across the table to cover her hand with his.

"Yes. But my life is in New York, just as yours, is in California."

"I suppose so," he mumbled under his breath. "Would you care to dance?"

"I'd love to," she responded.

He drew her into his arms as they moved to the slow jazzy tune. His cheek rested against her hair. "Um-m," he moaned. "You feel good next to me."

Ignoring the sensual statement, she said, "The music is relaxing."

"Margaret? Is there someone, a man? In New York?"

"I date if that's what you mean. Why?"

"It's not important now."

They returned to their table, just as the meal was served. Margaret found the food delectable. Throughout the evening, they enjoyed playful repartee.

Later standing outside her door, she whispered, "It was a lovely day. Thank you." If only we could stay this happy forever she thought.

"Thank you for sharing it with me," Grant replied. His lips engaged hers for a brief moment Margaret couldn't be sure it happened. Before she could respond he turned and retreated, moving along the beach line.

A pang of disappointment covered Margaret. She anticipated several possibilities, but nothing like this. He failed to express any desire to linger over a drink. He'd left as if chased by demons. Why? He thinks you're a woman of easy virtue. It's a summer affair, you will soon forget she reasoned.

She pondered while she lay in bed that night. He will steal your heart then toss it aside. The remainder of her stay, Margaret planned to see him but he would not dominate her time. She was here to sort matters out as to why she ran out on her marriage ceremony. Poor Phillip!

Even as sleep claimed Margaret that night, Grant continued to control her thoughts. There must be a woman in Grant's life, someone special in California. Perhaps there were several women. Slick men with polished lines think nothing of toying with the affections of a woman. He's a gigolo. What a fool she was! She knew little about him. How could she be so irresponsible to forgo her traditional values?

When morning reared its head, Margaret felt as though she solved the national deficit. She decided her course of action. Humming, she descended the stairs, and met her aunt at the bottom step.

"How was your date with Grant?"

"Oh, that … fine," was the perfunctory reply. "A causal date like the rest. Besides, I leave for New York soon."

Kay shook her head in disbelief. "Your mother called earlier. I told her you were out late last night. Elisia seems anxious to speak with you."

"Oh, really? I hope nothing is wrong." Margaret paused.

~****~

"Hello, sir. May I help you?" the woman asked as she opened the door.

"Is this the Clark residence?"

"Yes, sir."

"I'm a friend of Margaret Stewart's. I believe she's visiting her aunt. My name is Phillip Johnson. May I come in?"

At this moment, Kay and Margaret entered the front room to inquire of the visitor at the door.

"Hello, Margaret," Phillip greeted.

Silence ensued.

"You might be more enthusiastic to see me," Phillip scolded. "I've traveled a long way to be with you."

"You should have called," Margaret stammered.

"Your mother said she'd inform you, that I was on the way. Did she forget to telephone?" Phillip queried.

"No, please forgive me. It's good to see you, Phillip," Margaret said as she moved forward, kissing his cheek. Mistaking her intention, Phillip opened his arms. His lips took proprietary possession of hers.

Puzzled, Kay observed the couple in total confusion.

"Darling, I've missed you terribly," Phillip said huskily. "I couldn't wait to see you."

"And I, you," Margaret said slowly, turning. "Phillip, this is my dearest aunt, Kay Clark.

Kay, meet Phillip Johnson. Phillip lives in New York, and we see one another socially.

"Socially?" Phillip countered in amazement.

"Make yourself comfortable, Phillip. I'm sure you're weary from the flight," Kay remarked.

"Yes, I am. Thank you."

"Mildred show Mr. Johnson to his room and help him settle in," Kay instructed. Shifting her gaze to Phillip, she said, "We'll have coffee when you return."

After Phillip exited the room, Kay stared mutely at Margaret.

"I can't believe he followed me here," Margaret commented, stunned. Kay's eyes engaged hers. "Okay, he's more than an acquaintance."

"I'm waiting," Kay chided.

"Kay, I ..."

Presently Phillip joined them. Margaret shrugged her shoulders in a helpless gesture. "I'm glad to be here. I thought the plane would never land." Phillip lowered himself in a chair and lifted the coffee cup to his lips.

"Tell me about yourself, Phillip," Kay said with sincerity. A mischievous smile played on her face.

Phillip exchanged meaningful glances with Margaret, then said, "I see Margaret hasn't mentioned me, nor our relationship."

"Phillip!"

"She's entitled to know the reason I'm here. Margaret and I met in college. We've known one another for five years. It was two years before she took me seriously. Nonetheless we've dated for three. A week before she left New York, I proposed. I love your niece Mrs. Clark," Phillip explained.

Perplexed, Kay listened with renewed interest. She saw her niece in a new light.

"Margaret claimed she needed time to put her life in focus. And she promised to give me an answer when she returned."

"Well, Margaret is tight-lipped," Kay replied. "Why don't you show Phillip around the island? I have a million things to do at the restaurant."

Phillip's unexpected arrival complicated the situation. Unable to respond, Margaret maintained a slumped posture. Her mind raced for what to say or do. "Phillip would you care to go for a swim?"

"What's this all about," Phillip challenged, a painful look worked on his face.

"I can explain everything."

Phillip leaned back in the chair. "This I've got to hear."

"Don't be angry with me, Phillip," Margaret replied, her eyes pleading with him to understand.

"Why haven't you mentioned me to your aunt?" Phillip asked in exasperation. "Why do you persist in this charade? You know how I feel about you, Margaret." He advanced on her.

"I'm confused, Phillip," she admitted. "You're making demands that I cannot fulfill. If you love me, be patient." Margaret turned her back to him. "Or leave me."

He recognized her determined stance. Phillip hesitated, collecting his thoughts. He had not expected honesty, her response threw him off balance. He would learn patience if it killed him.

"The swim sounds great. I'll be down shortly," he responded as he left the dining room.

"Margaret, my girl, there's more to you than meets the eye," Kay said whimsically."What will you tell Grant?" Margaret remained silent. "You do remember him?"

"Of course I do." Margaret paused, a quizzical expression on her face. "I'm not sure."

"Good luck, Margaret. You're gonna need it," Kay laughed as she went out the door.

What was she to do? Calm down Margaret told herself. She wasn't engaged to Phillip any longer, and Grant had no claims on her. It was a summer romance that ran out of control. Remain rational she told herself the situation will work out. Dismissing her dilemma she ran upstairs to change into her swimsuit.

"I think you'll enjoy St. Raphael's," Margaret said as they strolled along the beach. "Life is unhurried here. One could grow accustomed to the flow."

"Why do you act as though someone is following you?" Phillip asked curiously. "You seem edgy."

"Don't be silly."

He selected a spot and they began to unpack the picnic supplies. Afterward he turned to take Margaret in his arms. At first she resisted, alas she relented to his show of affection.

Phillip traveled a great distance to be with her and she had behaved poorly, this he could not understand and this troubled him.

His stocky frame of medium height, a fair complexion, blonde hair and blue eyes was that of a patient and kind man. His lips were tenderly urging and coaxing her to relax her posture. He had been patient for three years; he never asked more than she could give. Phillip would be a sensitive, considerate and loving husband Margaret told herself. He could provide a secure lifestyle. His law practice began slowly and after five years was successful. If she had one ounce of sense she would marry Phillip and return to New York.

It was a beautiful day with a brilliant cobalt sky dotted with cumulus clouds. Phillip's boyish vulnerability shined in his smile. She couldn't decide what changed about him but soon she began to relax.

They swam for awhile then stretched out on the sand to rest.

"How about a diet coke?" she offered

"Sounds good."

"How will your practice survive while you're away?" Margaret asked.

"Since I've recently hired an associate, I suspect, fine," he said with a satisfied smile. "You're beautiful if not more so with a tan."

"Well, thank you."

"How are you really, Margaret? Have you decided what you want out of life?"

"I'm feeling more peaceful than I have in a long time. Being here has been good for me. As far as what I want ..."

If her tone was any indication, Phillip suspected he wouldn't like her response. Heaving a deep sigh he said, "No matter. Let's enjoy one another," he murmured.

Margaret's expression changed to one of relief.

~****~

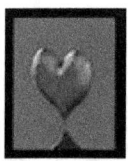**Chapter 5**

Last night Grant became overwhelmed with fear, he panicked. No closer to insight of his emotions he would maintain his distance and forget her. He told himself that he would find it hard to settle for one woman. Eventually he would tire of Margaret like the rest. Bill was right in his assumption. It was impossible for him to be faithful to one woman not to mention the threat to his career should he marry.

Marry? That will be the day!

Grant suspected today would be a lost day. Ordinarily when he was troubled he would retreat into seclusion. He started to clean the beach house. Perhaps this would distract him.

~****~

With anticipation Kay waited for the confrontation. Life had taken an added flavor since Margaret's arrival in St.

Raphael, Kay mused. She knew there would be an explosion when Grant met Phillip.

Tonight Phillip and Margaret dined at the club. With the exception of meeting Peter and Tonya, the evening was a success. Instinctively, Margaret disliked Tonya. Phillip dismissed the scene as inconsequential, although Margaret noticed the agitation he tried to conceal as he grasped her elbow and ushered her from the club. The tension lessened between them as the two walked slowly along the beach.

"Who is Grant?" Phillip asked disdainfully. He had to quell the mounting anxiety.

"Just someone I met a few weeks ago." She hoped he wouldn't pursue the subject.

"Peter made it sound as though the two of you were an item?"

"Peter and Tonya like to start trouble," Margaret coaxed. "I wouldn't take either of them seriously."

"I'm sure you're correct in your assumption," he replied. By this time, his mood had mellowed. "When will you return to New York?"

"In less than two weeks."

"You know how I feel about your Margaret. Come back with me?"

"When will you leave?"

"Two or three days at the most. We can be married next week."

"Be patient with me, Phillip. We've waited this long, another week's not asking much. I promise I'll have an answer for you when we return to New York. You wouldn't want to marry me unless I'm sure."

Sighing, he whispered, "I'm exhausted. Good night, love."

She noticed his eyes momentarily reflected hurt. Phillip was sweet. She disliked putting him off, but she couldn't decide. The next two days they played golf and sailed. She enjoyed his company and hadn't realized how much she missed him.

Margaret hadn't heard from Grant in three days. Obviously he met the challenge and he had no further interest in her. Come to think of it, she reacted in a similar manner to the men she had dated in the past. Her mother warned, "One day you will meet a man who will affect you like no other, and he'll treat you in the same manner. When he leaves, a part of you will go with him." Strange how the thought came to mind.

Kay prepared a farewell dinner for Phillip. He would leave for New York in the morning. Kay wondered why Grant disappeared and was amazed Phillip's visit had been pleasant.

~****~

Grant was surprised when Tonya appeared at his doorstep. She explained, she happened to be in the neighborhood. As the night progressed one thing led to another.

Waking with Tonya the next morning, Grant couldn't remember a thing. The night before was a total blur. He suspected the alcohol affected him more than usual. Tonya eluded he had been a good lover. He couldn't dispute this because his memory failed him. Grant recalled Tonya had mentioned she saw Margaret with Phillip somebody. Experience taught him never to take things at face value, especially with Tonya. Nevertheless his curiosity was piqued.

He wanted to see Margaret. On a whim he dressed and started for the Clark home. After ringing the bell, he waited. Grant expected Mildred to answer, just the same he was stunned to see a man answer the door.

"Yes?" Phillip queried.

"Good evening, I'm Grant Michaels. Is Margaret in?"

"Are you expected?" Phillip asked, sizing up the situation.

"Not exactly."

"I suggest you forget Margaret, pal." Phillip smiled through thinned lips.

"I'm not your pal." Grant scowled.

"I'm her fiancée, Phillip. I'll tell her you dropped by."

"Was that the doorbell, Kay?" Margaret questioned from the kitchen.

"Mildred will get it," Kay remarked. "This will be the best meal he's ever had. Incidentally, I like that young man of yours."

"I'm glad you approve, but I haven't agreed to marry him."

"Do you want to be an old maid?"

"No, I want to be sure of my decision," Margaret reminded.

The meal was a success. Phillip had an early flight scheduled tomorrow, in lieu of this everyone retired at ten.

Margaret saw Phillip off the following day. She entered the living room, just as Kay directed her attention to the newspaper.

"Will you look at this! I don't believe it!"

"What … believe what?" Margaret queried.

"The picture on the front page," Kay said as her index finger tapped the newspaper.

Margaret directed her attention to the front page and stared in disbelief. She was aghast.

"I thought he looked familiar. Now we know why. He's Grant Michaels, the Hollywood actor. Imagine a movie star in our midst and we didn't even realize it," Kay marveled. "Who's the beautiful woman?"

Margaret experienced a maelstrom of emotions: surprise, shock, anger and disappointment.

"It says, she's the woman in his life, Nina Albright. She's an actress."

Margaret managed to overcome the initial shock. Her anger began to escalate. Taking a deep breath she leaned closer to inspect the picture. He looked absorbed with the woman as they departed a night club his arm wrapped possessively around her. How could she have been a fool? Why had he taken advantage of her? She had been so eager, willing and easy. What a dimwit. Now he didn't know her name. She should have heeded her instincts about Grant.

~****~

Grant played the scenario over and over in his head. Margaret's engaged. She had toyed with his emotions, won his trust, to satisfy some female pervasive need. When really it had been a game to her. Maybe one last fling before she tied the knot?

The women in Grant's life had been docile. He'd always been the one to break it off Grant reminded himself. Some how this did not satisfy his wounded pride. She had fooled him completely. Unaccustomed to capricious women, he was astounded. Grant prided himself on never making promises he couldn't deliver. He pleasured many women and had enjoyed the pleasure they were more than eager to offer. But, he had not deceived them like the devious Margaret Stewart.

He was aware women like her existed, but he hadn't experienced one first hand. Margaret would leave soon and he would never see her again. Given this, he would avoid her as much as possible. Grant glanced at the clock, four o'clock. He brought a hand to his chin and was greeted by the stubble of a day's beard. He had not bathed nor shaved today. This was ridiculous! Grant had brooded all day. After a shower and shave, Grant dressed and began to straighten the beach house. He would go for a swim afterward he considered. The telephone rang.

"Hello?" Grant said, lifting the receiver.

"Grant?" a female voice questioned.

"Yes, Anna," he responded, raking a hand through his moist dark hair.

"I understand you're in St. Raphael's for the summer," Anna began.

"Yes. What's up?" Grant asked with concern. He recognized the troubled tone in her voice. Anna and Grant had been confidantes since childhood.

"I need a fresh perspective. Can I stay with you for while?"

"What's wrong, Anna?" Grant queried impatiently.

"Everything," Anna said evasively. "Can I come?" Grant heard her voice crack on the verge of tears.

"When will you leave?" he asked calmly.

"In the morning," Anna uttered, her voice tinged with happiness. "Thank you, Grant. I knew you would understand."

"I'll meet your plane."

Anna told him when she'd arrive and rang off. She had always been the strong one, together and never giving up. If Anna fell apart, this must be terrible he thought. They had always consoled one another. Truth was, his sister comforted him most times. He wouldn't let her down.

Opening the door, Grant moved outside. The ocean always seemed to sooth him. This was the life he thought as his view scanned the azure sky and cobalt water - paradise. He threw a towel into a nearby chair and started for the water. With broad strokes, Grant glided through the water, luxuriating in the comfort it provided. Exercise had been a refuge for his troubled spirit.

What troubled Anna? Regardless, Grant would lend her solace.

His lifestyle grated on him. What would he do? He'd been an actor so long he knew nothing else. His mind searched for answers.

An hour later Grant made for shore. Breathing rapidly he lowered himself on a lounge chair. Difficult though it was, he tried to forget Margaret. Grant couldn't focus on anything else. He wanted to confront her and demand an explanation. Surely he deserved this.

Clad in jeans and a navy sport shirt, Grant strode purposefully toward the Clark home. He practiced several approaches as he walked briskly along the beach line. The honest, direct approach would be best. His knuckles contacted the door. Moments later, Mildred opened the door. Grant struggled to hide his anger.

"Hello, Mildred," Grant greeted with his best smile."May I come in?"

"Yes, sir," Mildred responded as she stepped aside.

"Is Margaret in?" Grant asked. Mildred's wary expression disturbed him. Perhaps they had had a laugh at his expense.

"Please have a seat," Mildred offered with a gesture of her hand. "I will be right back."

Mildred's behavior was peculiar he thought. Moments later Kay joined him in the living room.

"What brings you here?" Kay remarked, assessing his mood.

His face was without expression. "Where's Margaret?"

"Would you care for coffee or iced tea?" Kay parried.

"No, thanks," Grant replied."Mildred's acting strange. What's happening?"

"Margaret didn't mention Phillip?" Kay questioned cautiously.

"I know about her fiancée," Grant ground out. "You didn't answer my question!"

"She's not here," Kay blurted.

"I'll wait," Grant responded with acrimony.

"Margaret's gone. She on her way to New York," Kay murmured. "I'm sorry."

"She did? When?"

"This afternoon," Kay cajoled as she placed a hand on his shoulder. "Margaret's confused."

"That's great! She leaves without a word," Grant growled.

"Maybe it's better this way," Kay said sympathetically.

~****~

Grant met the amphibian plane early the next day. Anna was drawn in appearance.

"Thanks for letting me come," Anna said moving from of his embrace.

"Don't mention it." He shrugged his shoulders in a helpless gesture. "C'mon, I'll show you the house."

"I can see why you came here for the summer," Anna commented. "It's heaven on earth."

"I rest my case," Grant laughed. He knew Anna was putting on a front, he would wait until she was ready to talk about it. He opened the patio doors, a wonderful breeze blew through the beach house.

Anna exclaimed about the panoramic view and how much she loved the house. Grant carried her bags upstairs and sat them in the guest room.

"When you're ready, Anna come downstairs and we'll have iced tea." Grant winked, and turned to depart.

While she unpacked he would prepare the tea. He sensed a familiar long session in store similar to the ones they used to have. With Anna visiting he wouldn't have time to think about Margaret.

For this, Grant was grateful. Hearing Anna's footsteps, Grant turned and smiled.

"Let's go into the living room, we'll be more comfortable," Grant offered, passing Anna a cold glass. He lowered himself beside her on the sofa. "How was the trip?" he asked congenially.

"You don't have to make pretenses for my sake," Anna murmured.

"What's wrong?"

"You name it," Anna muttered, her gaze shifted to the glass in her hand. Tears filled her eyes, as she looked up.

"Start at the beginning."

"You know the promotion, I told you about?" Anna began.

"I remember."

"Well, I didn't get it. The boss's son – the weasel, got it."

"It happens all the time," Grant reasoned."I'm sorry, but it's no reason to fall apart."

"That's just the beginning," Anna cried as she lifted the napkin beneath her drink to dry her tears.

"There's more?"

"Much more," she sniffled. "Ben wants a divorce."

Grant moved closer, draping an arm around her shoulders. "What's happened?"

"You know the way I am about my work. Well he said, he wants a wife not a career woman. It seems I don't spend enough time with him." Anna threw herself into his arms. Tears fell with increased rapidity.

Grant held her close. Anna's life fell apart and she sought him in her hour of need, Grant considered. "He's willing to throw in the towel after ten years?"

"That's what I said," she sniffled.

"What will you do?"

"I need time to think," Anna responded. "That's why I'm here."

"Are you sure there's no way to reconcile this with Ben?" Grant queried.

"He's involved with his secretary." Anna burst into tears once more.

"Forget the son-of-a-gun!" Grant would throttle Ben Jacobson, but good.

He held her until she ran out of tears.

"You're better off without him," Grant cajoled.

"When this happened, you were the first person I thought of." Anna forced a smile.

"We've always helped each other over life's hurdles." Grant lifted Anna's chin with his thumb. "Now, no more tears. Where's the old spirit?" Anna smiled. "That's my girl."

"What shall we do for dinner?" Anna asked. "I'm starved."

~****~

**Chapter 6**

"Oh, you are?" Grant teased."You must be feeling better."

"Yes. Thanks to you."

"I'm taking you to dinner. We'll dance and forget our troubles. Deal?"

Anna nodded. "Of course."

~****~

Kay remembered last night as though it just happened. The expression on Grant's face, she would never forget. Surely Margaret was taught better. Kay never meddled in other's lives, in any event she felt like thrashing Margaret.

Life came easy to Margaret. Her niece was blessed with beauty, brains, wealth and the ability to drive men crazy. Most women were grateful to find a man to love, but Margaret had two. Kay realized Grant was dishonest with Margaret but he loved her, she realized. She would never forget the look on his face and her own sense of helplessness. Youth was wasted on the young Kay thought.

~****~

"You're lucky. I'm your brother, otherwise you'd be in trouble," Grant teased as Anna whirled before him.

"I'm glad you approve."

Anna accepted the hand Grant extended to her. "Shall we?" She looked gaunt but her makeup successfully hid the circles under her eyes Grant considered. He would do his best to help her forget.

"What a nice club," Anna remarked as they entered *Maggie's*. "It's airy and comfortable; yet private."

"The owner's proud," Grant added.

A hostess escorted them to a table with a spectacular view. The combo returned and jazz bellowed throughout.

"Would you care for a drink before dinner?" the waitress offered.

"I'll have a rum and coke," Anna ordered.

"A scotch and water," Grant muttered as the waitress's gaze shifted to him.

"Coming right up." Briefly the waitress wrote on her pad and turned to take her leave.

"I'm glad to be with you, Grant," Anna said softly. Grant leaned closer. It was difficult to hear over the music.

"What?" he questioned.

She covered his large hand on the table with hers. "I suspected, I needed this. And to be with you," Anna answered.

"What are brothers for?"

Kay stood in the background but she witnessed the tender exchange. Sadly, she misjudged Grant. The little number with him, was new to the island Kay thought. He sure made friends fast. How could she have misjudged him? He's an actor Kay conceded to the small voice within.

Grant was the perfect host throughout the meal. They talked about old times – their first loves. Anna needs a distraction Grant thought. It was good to protect someone; to care. They danced and laughed until both grew weary. A short time later they started for the beach house. Tonight he enjoyed himself. She helped him to forget as well.

"How do you amuse yourself when you're not entertaining a wayward sister?"Anna asked with an appreciative smile."You haven't mentioned Margaret once."

Grant stopped dead in his tracks. Anna had not missed the abrupt change. The air became tense between them. He stood, his hands clenched, his jaw set firmly as his brows came together in a frown. Moments later, he said, "I don't want to talk about it." He turned his back to her.

"Did I say something wrong?" Anna asked, concern lacing her voice.

He heaved a sigh, and turned to face her, a smile on his face. "I'm sorry." Grant leaned to kiss her cheek. "C'mon."

Puzzled Anna allowed the subject to drop. She considered this a sore subject.

"Thank you, Grant." Anna stood on tip-toes to kiss his cheek. "Sleep well."

~****~

Two days prior, Margaret returned to her apartment in New York. She collected her cat, Popcorn, from her parents and began to settle into her routine. Her early arrival would allow her ample time to do chores. Popcorn was pleased to see her. He arched his back and rubbed against her while his tail stood rigid similar to an antennae. She loved the short-hair, white cat with black spots. He was a gift from her parents. Margaret explained that her early return was prompted because her apartment was in need of a major clean-up. Her parents accepted the explanation without further question.

Disquieted, Margaret was dressed in faded jeans and one of her father's old shirts as she glanced around her loft apartment. The hardwood floors needed polishing, the cupboards rearranging after new shelf paper, and the closets begged for attention. When she opened a closet objects or boxes would fall out. In the past she would push them inside and close the door. Now it was time to organize her life.

Kay expressed her disapproval of Margaret's decision to runaway. She suggested Margaret confront Grant with his deceit. Kay had always supported her efforts in the past. This was different, Kay clearly thought Margaret was a coward. She was, Margaret conceded.

Grant was deceitful from the start. Margaret could not abide a relationship based on dishonesty. Given this, she would fall for a gigolo. She would not settle for this lifestyle. She valued stability, security and direction. A man would come along eventually who fit the description. She was a successful business woman; independent. She would be fine. Suddenly she relished the thought of finding someone to love, who would be a companion, and share her life. Alas there was Phillip to consider Margaret reflected.

Phillip left several messages on her answering machine when he discovered she had returned to New York. As yet, Margaret failed to return his calls. Over the next few days she would contemplate the situation.

"What do you think, Popcorn?" Margaret asked the cat at her feet.

"Meow?"

Margaret shook her head in dismay.

The next two hours she laid shelf paper in the pantry. Neatly arranging its contents. Fifties-to-sixties music bellowed from the radio as she worked.

Exhausted by late afternoon, she sank into a chair after pouring herself a glass of iced tea. She was a physical wreck but she felt better. Given this, she broke two fingernails in the process. Small price to pay she mused.

The telephone rang. She took a large swallow of her tea, before answering the telephone. "Hello?"

"Margaret darling, how are you?" Phillip greeted. "Did you get my messages?"

"I've been busy. I'm sorry I haven't had time to return your call. I'm fine. How are you?"

"Anxious to see you. Have dinner with me?"

" How about we order take-out?" Margaret volunteered.

"I'm game," Phillip responded. "What time?"

"Sevenish. I thought we'd order a large pizza. Maybe you could pick up some beer on the way?" Margaret suggested enthusiastically.

"No problem." Phillip rang off.

It would be great to see Phillip again. Margaret had her fill of solitude. She would handle this delicately. Pushing up, she padded to the bathroom. A glimpse of her reflection in the mirror indicated a grubby face and stringy hair. A bath was in order.

Once outside the shower, she leaned through the doorway to glance at the clock in her bedroom, six o'clock. Leisurely she applied her makeup, dressed in jeans and a turquoise pullover. At six-thirty she telephoned a nearby delicatessen for a large pizza.

Phillip arrived promptly at seven with the pizza and beer in hand.

"I asked them to deliver it," Margaret said as she took the box from him.

"The delivery man came just as I arrived," Phillip explained. He kissed her cheek.

"Come in," she said with a gesture of her hand.

Once inside they settled in the living room on the sofa. Margaret had the dvd player poised and ready for the movie.

"It's good to see you again," Phillip said as his gaze scanned the pizza, beer and the woman at his side.

"I'm glad to be back in New York," Margaret chimed in. "I thought we could watch my favorite old classic, *Lost Horizon*."

"That's great. It's one of my favorite movies," Phillip said as he pointed the remote control and turned on the movie. "I've always liked Ronald Coleman and Jane Wyatt."

Both enjoyed easy conversation and settled into watching the classic movie.

~****~

Anna woke in good spirits the next morning. It was wonderful to feel relaxed. She needed this badly. Grant had shown her a wonderful time.

The telephone captured Anna's attention. It rang several times. Where was Grant?

"Hello?" Anna greeted.

"Anna?" Judith Michaels queried.

"Yes, momma."

"Thank goodness you're alright! When I found out what happened, I tried everywhere to reach you," Mrs. Michaels rattled off.

"I'm okay. I had to getaway, to think," Anna explained. Pushing her black hair off her face, Anna sat up in bed. "You understand."

"I can't imagine what's got into Ben," Mrs. Michaels chided."He has a lovely home, a beautiful wife, and now this."

"I know." Anna's voice cracked.

"How are you?" her mother asked cautiously.

"Don't worry, momma. I'll work this through," Anna began. "Grant's been sweet."

"You've been close since you were children. I thought I would find you with him."

"I didn't mean to worry you."

"I know. Have you made plans yet?"

"No," Anna answered flatly. "Could we change the subject?"

"Of course. How's your brother."

"He's been a perfect host," Anna voice brightened. "Although …" she paused.

"He's not ill?"

"He's fine."

"Well?"

"I think he's carrying a torch for someone," Anna offered. "I haven't convinced him to talk about it. But I will."

"I hope he finds a nice girl and settles down. Anyway he's not getting any younger," her mother responded. "Is Grant there?"

"Don't mention anything I've said to Grant?" Anna cautioned. "Let me handle it."

~****~

"*Lost Horizon* never fails to inspire me. It gives one hope. I would love to be in Shangri La," Margaret said, stretching.

"That's a fact," Phillip conceded. He drew her into his arms.

Margaret reached a decision. She would give Phillip a chance. She had known him a long time. He would be a good husband. She relaxed in his embrace.

Phillip's mouth crushed down on hers. Margaret tensed, for a moment she imagined Grant's face. She shook herself mentally. Consciously she tried to enjoy the kiss. His mouth became demanding. His hand moved over her body.

"I've gone out of my mind," Phillip rasped. "I need you, tonight," His hand arched over her breasts.

Before she could react he lowered her on the sofa. Pressing his length to hers, Phillip forged ahead. He trailed kisses along her neck to the soft skin exposed over her bra.

"Phillip ... please."

"I love you, Margaret."

Somehow she had to stop him, without hurting his pride. Margaret felt numb. She should feel passion, desire his touch, but ...

"Not, now! Phillip, please." Where had that come from? Margaret wondered. The words were short and clipped as she pushed him away.

Frustrated and angry, Phillip rose slightly. His frown was evident as his eyes searched hers. "What do you mean? Not now?" Phillip questioned suspiciously.

"I can't." Margaret lowered her eyes, preening herself. "I'm sorry."

"Damn it! Come clean with me, Margaret."

"I promised an answer, but I just don't know."

"I'm not about to sit around and wait for the tidbits you bestow," Phillip threatened."What do you want from me?"

Silence.

"I love you Margaret. I've asked you to marry me. But I won't be put off much longer," he warned as he rose from the sofa. "Give it, some serious thought." The door closed quietly behind him.

Tears filled Margaret's eyes. Much later she fell asleep.

Friday afternoon Margaret was unsuccessful in putting Grant from her mind. Phillip's kiss failed to fill her with passion, the way Grant's had. This would serve no purpose, Grant had lied to her. When Phillip pressed his body against hers, she unconsciously thought of Grant. His memory taunted her. Each day Grant filled her thoughts. At night, oh, what fantasies. She told herself the foolishness had to end.

Lifting the receiver, Margaret punched out the number.

"Marlowe, Johnson and Phipps," a secretary queried.

"I'd like to speak with Phillip Johnson."

"Whom shall I say is calling?" the secretary screened.

"Margaret Stewart."

"One moment please."

She drummed her fingers on the kitchen counter top. Margaret had made her decision.

"Margaret?" Phillip's deep voice answered.

"Yes, Phillip," Margaret said with a deep intake of breath. "I've decided to marry you."

Silence prevailed for several moments.

"Did you hear me?" Margaret asked in disbelief.

"I thought my ears deceived me," Phillip muttered finally. "I can't believe it."

"It's true."

"That's wonderful, darling. Have lunch with me?"

"I've agreed to have lunch with mother. We're going shopping afterward. A girl's day out. You understand?"

Margaret hadn't missed the pleased tone in Phillip's voice with her announcement.

"That's fine. We'll have dinner?"

"Of course." She laughed.

"I'll pick you up at eight. Wear the dress I like." Phillip rang off.

At least her emotions ceased to vacillate. She would tell her mother at lunch.

Margaret met her mother, Elisia Stewart, an articulate woman inside the small restaurant near Bloomingdale's.

"It's good to see you," Elisia Stewart said embracing her daughter.

"Thank you mother."

"Come, I'm famished." Elisia turned and gestured to the hostess.

Moments later they were seated, "You might have hired someone to do the cleaning and reorganizing," Elisia scolded.

"We haven't seen much of you. Your father wants to know when you will visit and not blow through as the wind?"

"Soon mother," Margaret murmured. "How's your salad?"

"It's wonderful. I love the little shrimp on top," Elisia said, lifting her glass of water. After scanning the room, Elisia's gaze settled on her daughter. "You look gaunt. What's wrong Margaret?"

"Nothing, mother."

"A mother knows her child better than anyone. Since you've returned from the Caribbean, you haven't been the same. I thought vacations were supposed to be good for one?"

Margaret recognized the stubborn expression on her mother's face. She knew Elisia wouldn't relent until she answered truthfully.

"If you refuse to confide in me, Kay will."

"You've talked to aunt Kay," she accused. Elisia shook her head, a troubled expression played on her face.

"I met this man ..." Margaret began.

"You're in love with him!"

"No," she denied, leaning closer. "Lower your voice."

"It's heaven sent. Never thought I would see the day!" Elisia exclaimed, oblivious to everyone's eyes on them.

"You don't have to be so happy about it," Margaret said crossly.

"It's wonderful darling," Elisia beamed. "Who's the man that's stolen your heart?"

"Grant Michaels. Before you get excited, cool your jets, mom."

"It's not unrequited love?" Elisia queried. A serious note entered her voice. Margaret shook her head. Puzzled, Elisia stared at her daughter.

"I'm not sure it's anything."

"You can do better than that Margaret Elisia Stewart," Elisia remarked in her best parental voice.

"It was a summer romance, mother. That's all." Margaret's eyes settled with feigned interest on her chef's salad.

"You're not pregnant?" Elisia challenged.

Inhaling and exhaling audibly, Margaret ground out, "Hardly, mother. That's not the problem."

"That's a relief." Elisia released a deep sigh. "Why do you persist in looking so grim?"

"Don't concern yourself mother. I'm a big girl. The man is a philanderer. He lied to me. Besides I'll never see him again."

"Why?"

"Forget about that. I have some good news," Margaret said forcing enthusiasm into her voice for her mother's sake.

"I could use some good news," Elisia said absently.

"I'm marrying Phillip Johnson."

Elisia almost choked on her glass of white wine. She swallowed hard and said incredulously, "What?"

"It's true. Mother, it's time I stopped fantasizing about Mr. Right and was practical," Margaret confessed.

"Why would you marry a man you don't love?" Elisia asked with wide eyes.

"A woman needs a stable man, security and children. Romance is fine but I'm realistic. Phillip is a good man and he loves me. In time, I'll grow to love him. I can't afford to indulge myself with rogues. You still have to wake up the next morning in the real world."

"Are you sure?"

"My mind is set."

"When will you and Phillip marry?"

"We're having dinner tonight to discuss it," Margaret assured. She reached across the table and squeezed her mother's hand.

~****~

"It's beautiful, Phillip. And much to large," Margaret said in amazement.

"It's a carat size diamond, Margaret. I hope you like the Marquis setting," Phillip said, placing the engagement ring on her finger.

Phillip kissed her. "My parents consider me the luckiest man on earth."

"I'll try to be a good wife," Margaret said with sincerity.

The next two weeks Phillip escorted Margaret to the opera, dinner and to several Broadway plays. Margaret struggled to transition into her new role.

Margaret concerned herself with great effort to banish Grant from her thoughts, but he continued to creep into them each morning and into her dreams at night. Instead of making love to Phillip, she imagined Grant. The man possessed not only her body, but her mind and heart as well. Would this never end? What a fate, to marry a man and dream of another. Was there no justice in life?

Phillip talked of his plans of where they would live, what they would do, children and a wife's duties to entertain clients. Margaret knew she should be excited but she felt empty inside.

Tonight Phillip stood her up. He claimed a client had an immediate problem. Just the same she was weary of the social scene. Was this the life she would settle for?

No! Her subconscious cried emphatically. Phillip didn't make her tingle, nor her stomach flutter with butterflies. One man had but it was hopeless to think something might come of it. He's a gigolo. Grant enveloped her in his web like a spider and spoiled her for other men. There could be no one else for Margaret of this she was certain. She would see Phillip for lunch tomorrow, then she would explain and call off the engagement.

"What was so important?" Phillip questioned after the waitress took their order. "It sounded urgent."

"I don't know where to begin."

"You're not getting cold feet?" he offered.

"In a way …"

"My parents will love you. There's nothing to be afraid of." Phillip patted her hand affectionately.

"Phillip, I can't go through with it," Margaret said with a determined expression. Lowering her eyes, "I'm sorry."

"You don't mean that. You have the jitters. Men usually develop them." Phillip attempted a soft laugh. "Come now, relax."

"I do. But not for the reason you think," Margaret began. "Please believe me."

His gaze fixed mutely on Margaret. "You're serious?"

"I'm fond of you Phillip, but I don't love you," she confessed. "You deserve better." She slipped the engagement ring off her finger and placed it in Phillip's hand.

"It's the guy on the island," Phillip said laconically.

Surprised by Phillip's astuteness Margaret nodded.

"You're in love with him."

"It's no use. Everyone at one time or another must endure the one who got away. I'll get over it."

"He dumped you?"

"He's a gigolo."

"I regret what I said, earlier," Phillip said softly. "I'll admit I'm unhappy about it. I suppose deep down I've always known we were just friends. At least you're honest and I respect you for it."

"Thanks for understanding."

"When will you return to work?" Phillip asked casually. He tucked the ring into the breast pocket of his jacket.

"Monday." Margaret forced a smile.

Lunch came and went. The conversation after her announcement was tense. Before this neither searched for words. In any event, one does not call off an engagement every day. She didn't know what possessed her to consent in the first place. Phillip was like a brother. Thank heaven she had the good sense not to follow through.

~****~

**Chapter 7**

It was Friday and Margaret would watch the late movie on television. *Rio Bravo*, a John Wayne film was scheduled tonight. Margaret loved John Wayne. She would eat, bathe and curl up with the Duke at ten o'clock she thought, gazing into the shops downtown. For two and half hours she had wandered through the crowded streets looking blankly at the window displays without really seeing them.

Of course Phillip accepted the news nobly, although she had not missed the painful expression behind the polite mask. Margaret hurt him deeply and she felt like a snake. She suspected when he had time to consider the matter, he would not speak to her again.

"Way to go Margaret!" she said aloud.

Popcorn was curled on the sofa when she returned home. He lifted his head and gazed through hooded eyes.

"I know how you feel," Margaret said to Popcorn. "Maybe a bath is the answer?"

She soaked in a rose-scented bubble bath, luxuriating in the relief the warm water provided her stressed muscles. With dinner out of the way, Margaret sat Indian style on the sofa with a bowl of popcorn in her lap waiting for the movie to start.

Several commercials came and went then a voice announced, "Our regularly scheduled movie will be replaced with Bachelor Party." Across the screen displayed the words: starring, Grant Michaels. Margaret's eyes riveted on the name. Moments later his handsome face flashed on the screen. He appeared younger, but Margaret would know his face anywhere. The myriad of emotions she struggled to forget surfaced. She would turn the movie off after a few minutes. Surely it wouldn't hurt to watch a few minutes of the movie?

~****~

Waking from a dream, Grant pushed a hand through his damp hair with a groan. The dream had been so vivid. Margaret's body was damp with perspiration as she lay beneath him. Grant heaved a deep sigh and shook his head. This was absurd!

She's not ruining my vacation," he told himself. He sat up in bed.

"Grant? You okay?" Anna called through the closed door.

"I'm fine."

"Are you ready for breakfast?" Anna asked cheerfully.

"I'll be out in a few minutes," Grant responded as he threw the covers back and stood.

"Ummm," he moaned as the water pelted his skin. A bath would revive him. He was pleased to have Anna here in St. Raphael's.

Clad in faded low-slung jeans and a blue polo shirt, Grant joined his sister for breakfast. Anna was good company. Time and conversation passed easily between them.

One area had been taboo in their conversation and this was Margaret, Anna thought. Every time she turned the conversation in this direction, he would become tense, refusing to answer her questions. Grant would utter an expletive under his breath, then become distant. Anna's curiosity was piqued.

Today Grant took Anna sailing and they snorkeled and swam as well. Although he loved seafood, Grant wasn't much of a fisherman. Anna thought it unusual for Grant to be moody. This was uncharacteristic of him.

~****~

Straddling a chair, Grant nodded. "It smells good."

"It's your favorite, French toast and bacon," Anna placed a portion of each to his plate. He smiled appreciatively. She would find out what bothered him if it was the last thing she did.

"Have you made any plans yet?" Grant asked casually.

"A few. I'll make them up as I go along," Anna joked.

"I'm glad you're feeling better," Grant smiled.

"Wish I could say the same about you."

"What is that supposed to mean?" he growled.

"You are restless and moody. Scarcely yourself."

"I'm sorry, Anna."

"You've changed. What's got into you, Grant?" Anna demanded.

No response followed.

"It's Margaret. You're in love with her. Why don't you go after her?"

"Have you spoke to Kay?"

A lucky guess Anna considered. She nodded.

"There's a small problem," Grant began. "She's engaged."

"What's it like little brother being on the other side?" Anna taunted.

"Lay off, Anna. I'm not in the mood."

"No confidence? Are you going to roll over and give up?" Anna knew if she baited Grant he would see fire and stop brooding.

"You don't get it, do you?" he barked. "She's getting married."

"Getting!" Anna let the word hang in the air.

"She never mentioned the other guy. I thought I meant something to her," he sneered. "She's just a tease."

"You're far from being an angel," Anna scolded. "How does she feel about you?"

"At first she was attracted to me. Who knows, now?" he left the sentence unfinished as if caught in his reverie.

"Well?"

"Now, I'm confused. She left without a word and failed to mention she had a fiancée. It's a hell of a way to find out," Grant glowered."I suppose, circumstances speak for themselves."

"Are you going to leave it at that?"

"I'm no fool. Obviously I don't mean anything or Margaret wouldn't have left," he reasoned. "It was just an affair. Now, it's over."

"Grant, I'm your sister," Anna reminded."Not one of those breathless admirers of yours."

His jaw set firmly. Anna recognized the fire reflected in his eyes. She realized he was an inch from choking her.

Grant rose. Although nervous, Anna sat calmly. Instead of approaching her, he turned and strode from the room.

Uncertain of his reaction, Anna sat in silence. She considered the rest was his problem. Anna heard Grant bumping around in the other room. A short time later the front door slammed. She accomplished what she planned. He no longer needed her. She started to pack for the return trip to California. It was time to move on with her life, and she was more than ready.

Grant strode along the beach uncertain of his destination. He had had more than enough of Anna. He was irked she had easily cut to the core of the matter. Grant had never chased a woman in his life and he wouldn't start now.

A number of women would love his attentions -- Tonya for one! Determined to enjoy his vacation he trekked onward.

After the third knock, Tonya answered the door.

"Grant!"

"May I come in?"

"Please." Tonya stepped back to allow him entry.

"Coffee?" she asked politely.

"No thanks."

"What's up?" Tonya queried.

"I know it's short notice, but would you like to go sailing?" He smiled expectantly.

"I'd planned a day with a friend," Tonya responded, her gaze moved upward in thought.

"I understand. Another time?" Damn, he was striking out with women nowadays.

"I could arrange a rain check," Tonya reassured. "I prefer to spend the day with you."

"Good. I'll pick you up at one." With a modified salute, he turned on his heel.

Tonya smiled to herself as she observed his retreating figure along the beach line.

~****~

"What are you doing?" Grant muttered as he stepped inside the beach house.

"I'm leaving," Anna announced.

"Why?" he asked, then paused. "I hope it's not because of our fight?"

"No, Grant. It's time I continued with my life."

"That's different." He exhaled deeply. "I'm going to miss you."

"Like the plague," she joked.

"Maybe just a little." He approximated his thumb and index finger together.

"Momma's right, you know," Anna baited.

"About what?" Grant knew he shouldn't ask however he went against his better judgment.

"It's time you married."

"I don't remember asking for a matchmaker." He kissed her cheek.

"Okay, I know when to butt out."

"When will you leave?"

"The flight is tomorrow morning."

"You should have told me sooner. I planned to take Tonya sailing today," Grant said with a mischievous gleam in his eyes.

"Business as usual," Anna said playfully. "You go ahead. I have some calls to make."

"You don't mind?"

"No, Grant. We can have dinner tonight. Go on and enjoy yourself. I'll be fine."

"See you tonight." He approached the stairs and turned at the first step. "I've enjoyed having you here."

"Me too," Anna responded. He climbed the stairs.

~****~

Tonya wore a bikini she knew emphasized her full figure. She would at last have a chance to win Grant for herself. Grant released a wolf whistle when she opened the door.

"I'm glad you approve."

"Who wouldn't?" Grant's gaze lazily perused her. "Ready?"

Nodding, she lifted her tote bag.

He flashed his best smile and moved a hand to the small of her back.

Aboard the *Westwind,* Grant prepared the sailboat to launch. A good day for sailing he thought the wind had picked up. Anna was right. It was time to take a definitive steps to resolve problems.

"You seem preoccupied." Tonya walked up behind him, drawing him to her.

In silence Grant looked over one shoulder to Tonya.

Nervous under his gaze, Tonya blinked. "The breeze feels so good. It's a marvelous day."

"I'm pleased you could join me," Grant said casually. He turned to face Tonya, embracing her.

"That looks like a good spot." Tonya pointed with one hand.

Grant flinched when Tonya selected a location he had taken Margaret. Suddenly the memory cut through him. He couldn't bring himself to share it with another. "There's a better one ahead."

He unloaded the raft and they boarded it for shore.

"The chicken's great," Grant complimented.

Tonya opened the Chignon Blanc and poured a glass for each. "To us," Tonya offered a toast.

"Cheers." He lifted his glass.

"I'm curious. Why did you ask me out?"

"What do you mean?"

"Until now you haven't given me a second thought," Tonya supplied, then waited for a response.

"Don't be silly." The words were hollow even to him.

"I know Margaret has gone."

"What has Margaret got to do with this?" Grant answered with a trace of irritation in his voice.

"Everything. You're seeing me on the rebound," Tonya challenged.

"How in the hell would you know?"

"I'm no fool. The reason I am here on vacation is to forget someone," Tonya responded in a whisper.

"Am I so transparent?"

"Only to everyone." Tonya laughed.

Both burst out in laughter.

"So tell me, what happened?" Grant queried.

"The man, I'm trying to forget?"

"Yes."

"It's a long story."

"We have the time."

"Unrequited love. Spicy enough for you?"

"I'm sorry."

"It's the story of my life," Tonya said sardonically."What about you?"

"I'm interested in Margaret Stewart. Unfortunately she's engaged."

"You see, we have something in common."

"Nevertheless we should enjoy ourselves," Grant added.

"Where do we go from here?"

"What do you want Tonya?"

"You. And to be happy," she purred.

"Let's start over."

Today, Grant realized the summer was over for him. The next few days he would prepare for the return trip to the States. Tonya was good company but no dice.

He spent the evening with Anna and they reminisced of pleasant times. Grant felt empathy for Tonya but everyone has problems he thought.

The following day Anna left for California. A pang of disappointment overcame Grant. He was through hiding. He would come to grips with the situation.

~****~

"It's good to have you with us, Mr. Michaels," the chauffeur said as he drove from the airport.

"Thank you, Caleb."

Silently, Caleb drove the Rolls-Royce Silver Cloud to the Bel-Air mansion. Grant was home at last! Uncertain where to begin Grant considered he would follow his instincts.

The servants exclaimed about his early arrival on August fifth. He remembered Tonya's confusion when he announced his plans to leave. Grant felt he needed familiar surroundings to help him solve his dilemma. He was numb inside.

The telephone rang several times. Where were the servants? Grant wondered.

He spoke gruffly on the telephone.

"What's happening, buddy?" Bill asked.

"I considered it time to return to civilization."

"I knew you would wise up about women."

"Love 'em and leave 'em," Bill said mischievously. "You're a lucky man, Grant."

Grant failed to see the humor. "How's that?"

"You have no responsibilities. Women think you're great." Bill paused for a moment. "No worries."

"You're the lucky one."

"You don't sound well. What's wrong?"

"Bill, I'm in big trouble," Grant explained, his voice slurred.

"I'll be right over."

Forty-five minutes later, Bill found Grant sprawled on the sofa. He couldn't believe his eyes. Grant hadn't shaved in a couple of days.

"What's happened?"

"Have a drink, pal," Grant coaxed.

"You're feeling sorry for yourself. I thought a vacation would be good for you."

"She's marrying someone else!" Grant blurted, as Bill helped him into bed.

"It's not the end of the world."

"Easy for you to say. You have the woman you want."

"We have to figure out how to get her back," Bill reasoned. "Margaret's an interior designer?"

"So what?"

"Use your imagination, my boy. Hire her to re-decorate your house." Before your career is over, Bill thought. The right woman could always turn a man sappy Bill reflected. He'd seen it many times.

Why hadn't he thought of it before? How would he go about the task? Grant wondered before sleep claimed him.

The seed was planted Bill thought, locking Grant's door as he departed.

~****~

**Chapter 8**

Grant woke with a terrible headache the next day. Every sound no matter how low pitched seemed amplified. He was miserable.

When Mrs. Michaels telephoned, Grant deliberately made an excuse to shorten the call. This obsession with Margaret Stewart had to stop. Why had he fallen victim to her charms? He speculated it was because she hadn't chased him like the others. Perhaps she represented a challenge? Whatever the reason he had to put an end to the nonsense. Bill obliged him by solving the problem.

He would telephone her.

Margaret tossed and turned after watching Bachelor Party. Merely going through the motions of living she returned to work.

There were several messages awaiting her when she returned to work. On the third day, Margaret had just stepped inside and kicked off her shoes when the telephone rang.

"Yes?" Margaret said impatiently.

"Hello, it's Grant. How are you?"

Suddenly her heart flew south for the winter. The last thing she expected was a call from Grant. Phillip maybe, but not Grant. "I'm fine, Grant. What a surprise."

He suspected she wouldn't make this easy. "Margaret, I have a job for you. Interested?"

"Work always interests me."

"I would like you to redecorate my home," Grant said blandly."Are you available?"

"There are several capable decorators in Beverly Hills," Margaret challenged.

"I want the best!"

"Of course, Mr. Michaels."

"Mr. Michaels?"

"What do you want Grant?"

"A decorator."

"Oh pl-ea-se ..." she drew the word out.

"If you don't need the business, fine, say so?" Grant prodded.

"I can refer you to -"

"I'll make it worth your while," he tempted. "Imagine, you can advertise that you've decorated Grant Michaels home. What rave reviews you'll receive."

Margaret considered his point for a moment. Grant knew how to bait her. She had hoped he would leave her alone.

"Okay, Grant," Margaret agreed.

"When will you leave for California?" Grant asked casually, twisting the telephone cord with one finger. "I'll pay for the flight."

"Of course," Margaret began. Hurriedly she worked to collect her thoughts. Should she really ask for trouble? she wondered.

"When may I expect you?"

"I have a few details to attend," Margaret said considering. "I'll leave in two days."

"Great. I'll have a ticket for you at the Atlanta airline terminal. See you soon." He rang off.

Why had she agreed to this absurd idea? It would be a feather in her cap she told herself, after all, Grant Michaels was a big name. Imagine the publicity! The telephone would ring from the posh set in Hollywood she mused. This would make her the envy of her competitors.

Margaret told Debra, who was her secretary about the new assignment. The necessary arrangements were made and Margaret prepared for departure.

Margaret almost backed out several times and returned to New York. Coward! She accused herself silently.

Caleb collected Margaret from the airport. The chauffeur informed her Grant had to work today. When they arrived at the Bel-Air mansion, Margaret was shown to her room.

Grant arrived home at nine o'clock worn out. He prepared a scotch and water and stepped out onto the patio to gaze at the stars. He always found it difficult to unwind after a long day. Grant summoned all the self restraint he could muster to keep from going straight into her room.

At ten o'clock the grandfather clock sounded. Grant decided to go for a swim. He hadn't bothered with a swimsuit. Who would know?

Margaret felt restless. It was a sultry night, maybe a swim would cool her off and allow her to sleep. She padded quietly downstairs.

Recklessly she slipped out of her swimsuit. Looking both ways, she saw no one around. She made a running leap and entered the lukewarm water. After a few laps of the pool, she began to relax in the moonlight.

Splash!

Now she was hearing things Margaret told herself. Her nerves were frayed. No further sound was heard. The water would relax her tension. Margaret drew in a deep breath before she dove under the water.

Contacting a solid object, Margaret halted. Frightened, she surfaced, gasping for air.

A warm body enveloped hers. It was strange, yet familiar in the darkness. Insistently a warm mouth captured hers. Startled she couldn't think only follow her instincts. His lips were demanding, tempting and urging her onward. Margaret was helpless as a familiar passion washed over her. Unable to refute his advances, she was drawn more and more into submission.

His large hands cupped her head and he moaned her name. Grant? She couldn't be sure this wasn't a dream.

Moments later, Grant's mouth covered one breast, awakening untold pleasures within Margaret. He felt her legs encircle his waist, drawing him closer. His arousal was obvious. Margaret surrendered. With a deep groan, he entered her. For several moments he did not move, only savored her soft, warm moistness.

"Oh, Margaret," he moaned. "I've missed you. Wanted you." She clung to him. Words were need less. Their bodies communicated their need. Hungrily his mouth moved over her body. His hands explored her secret places.

"Tell me, you want me," he coaxed. He moved against her in a slow rhythm, his breathing rapid and shallow.

"Oh, yes! That's it," she cried."I want you, Grant."

Grant's thrusts increased in depth and rhythm. Margaret was convinced this must be heaven.

"Oh, Grant … now," she moaned softly.

"Margaret, I can't control it's been a long time. Hold me."

She drew him closer, both were lost in the rapture.

Grant dipped under the water and pushed up gasping for breath. Several moments later his breathing slowed. His gaze riveted on Margaret.

"How could you?" she accused.

"I don't remember raping you."

"You ….you!" She was angry, she couldn't think straight.

"You loved every minute of it," Grant pointed out. She tried to push him away, but his grip prevented it. "Cut the innocent act!"

He loosened his grip on Margaret as her posture relaxed. Tenderly, Grant smoothed the hair away from her face. She brushed her lips against his. Grant's heart swelled.

For the past month, he had been thoroughly miserable. He had lived for this day. Grant's thoughts were geared on possessing this woman like no other. A surging inferno grew within him, demanding relief.

"Grant?"

"Sh-h-h. Love me," he whispered. "I've missed you."

Once again he took her to the heavens as she cried his name mindlessly.

"Yes!" he groaned as he thrust once forcibly then collapsed against her. "You belong to me."

Margaret delighted in their lovemaking, but she wouldn't allow him to regard her as a possession.

"This wasn't supposed to happen," Margaret began. "I -"

"But it has," Grant interrupted."We're meant for one another."

"No." Her nails dug into his shoulders as she pushed him away.

"You hell cat! You weren't fighting so hard a few minutes ago."

"Don't touch me!" she hissed.

"Oh now, you're indignant," Grant laughed incredulously. "You little hypocrite." Grant pulled her firmly to him. His mouth taking possession of hers."You witch, I've never wanted a woman like this."

"How touching," Margaret said icily."To ease your guilt you pretend I've led you on. How macho and convenient!"

"Hush, Margaret." Disgruntled, Grant hoisted himself on the side of the pool, then walked away without glancing over his shoulder.

Margaret was spellbound.

The next morning she considered she was thoroughly confused and frustrated, and lost control. She glanced at the clock, nine o'clock. Dismayed she slept late, Margaret jumped out of bed. Showering she reviewed last night's rendezvous with Grant. Until then, she was in control. Once more Grant managed to take the reins.

What would she say to him? she wondered. Margaret scrambled into a long dress of tee-shirt fabric. She loved the way it made her feel as though she wore nothing. Again she inspected her reflection and scurried from the room. The spiral staircase opened into a large foyer. Below the polished black and white marble floors glistened in the sunlight.

Anxiously she glanced around the house. The only sound was the occasional movement of pots and pans in the kitchen. Margaret walked toward the sound. Moving into the kitchen, she startled the cook preparing lunch.

"Oh, my," the older woman said under her breath. "Thought I lost my senses."

"I didn't mean to frighten you," Margaret apologized. She extended her hand to the older woman. "I'm Margaret Stewart. Mr. Michaels hired me to redecorate his home.

The older woman studied her for a long moment, then dried her hands on her apron and took Margaret's hand.

"I'd be Catherine, the cook. Have been with Mr. Michaels for ten years. I'm pleased to meet you, Ms. Stewart."

"Yes," Margaret acknowledged. "Where is he?"

"Left out, he did at six this morning," Catherine said as she shook her head.

"Work?"

"Indeed. When they start filming, he leaves early most days," Catherine replied. "C'mon, you must be hungry?"

"Yes, I am. Did Mr. Michaels leave a message for me?"

"First, you eat."

Margaret allowed Catherine to lead her onto the patio overlooking the pool. After she fussed over Margaret, Catherine served a large breakfast.

"You need to eat and get your strength. All that flying around wears one out. Here from New York, you are?"

"That's right." Margaret laughed. The older woman reminded her of a mother hen tending her young.

Margaret failed to clear her plate. The meal would feed two men Margaret thought. Her disapproval was more than apparent as Catherine gathered the dishes.

"What message did Grant leave?" Margaret prodded.

"He said you should have run of the house. Look around, jot down some ideas and he will discuss them with you tonight. He's expected for dinner," Catherine replied. Reaching inside her pocket, she removed a piece of paper. "Almost forgot to give you this."

Margaret accepted the note. It was sealed in an envelope that Catherine had folded in half.

"Thank you. Breakfast was good but the helping was to large. Usually I have toast and coffee."

"No wonder you're so thin." Catherine carried the tray into the kitchen.

Margaret opened the note and read:

Dear Margaret,

I'm sorry I couldn't be here this morning. I've written some ideas down. They are in study. I am pleased you are here. Thanks for the memorable evening. See you tonight.

Grant

She read the note several times. The nerve a memorable evening, huh? He was sated. The note riled her. Tonight she would be a cool number. So cold he would think he was in Siberia. Convinced she would be all business hereafter, she walked into the study.

She discovered the note pad on his desk. Sinking into the chair, she studied the list.

Grant Michaels had definite tastes. He was pampered and accustomed to his whims being catered. The household servants included an upstairs maid, housekeeper, cook and chauffeur, Catherine informed her.

Margaret browsed the spacious home most of the day making notes. A glimpse of her watch indicated five-thirty. Catherine would serve dinner promptly at six-thirty. Grant was expected at six.

Where had the afternoon gone? she wondered. The large house or estate had taken Margaret all day to review. The twenty rooms with seven baths, large kitchen not to mention tennis court and pool would be a challenge. Grant's bedroom was clearly masculine in appearance. The black lacquer Danish contemporary furniture indicated a man of breeding. But Margaret would improve it.

She would give his room a woman's touch – warmth and personality. So much for daydreaming Margaret thought, she had better go upstairs. She should bathe before dinner.

Pleased with her efforts Margaret glanced once more into the mirror. The lavender summer dress flattered her violet eyes. Had she gone lengths to please Grant? Well maybe a little.

Opening the door she stepped into the hallway. What was the weird sensation in her stomach? Butterflies? She struggled to appear confident as she moved downstairs, her blonde hair cascaded recklessly over one shoulder.

The maid dressed in a black and white uniform greeted her. "Good evening, miss. Dinner will be announced. Mr. Michaels is in the study. This way please." The servant opened the large, carved wood double doors.

"Thank you, Hilda. That will be all," Grant said glancing

up from his desk. Margaret moved forward. He continued to write for several moments, then pushed up from the desk. "Welcome to my home, Margaret," Grant greeted. "Care for a drink?"

"No, thank you," she replied. Margaret lowered herself in a nearby chair. "How was your day?"

"Not bad. But I'm always glad to make it home. What do you think?" he asked with a wave of his hand.

"Your home is gigantic. I've some ideas I hope you'll like," Margaret remarked brightly.

"Later. We'll have dinner, then discuss business."

"As you like."

"Good. You're even better looking by daylight." His predatory eyes scanned her appreciatively. He turned and removed a bottle of Perrier from a small refrigerator. Lifting the bottle to his mouth, he took a big swallow.

"Then you should be pleased," Margaret said, matter-of-factly. A knock at the door interrupted her sentence. Both shifted their gaze.

"Yes, Hilda?"

The door opened slightly as the servant leaned inside. "Sir, dinner is served."

"Thank you." Grant gestured with one hand for Margaret to precede him. "Shall we?"

She shot him an agitated look. Grant smiled, evidently pleased with himself. With an exaggerated smile, Margaret rose from the chair and walked out of the room.

"Manners now," he whispered as he fell into step beside her. "I don't recall you being so moody," he taunted as he pulled back her chair. Margaret lowered herself.

Instead of thanking him, she gave him a measured look.

He arranged himself across from her. The table was set formally with candlelight and a large centerpiece of freshly cut red roses and baby's breath artfully arranged. The room was bathed in a golden hue.

Hilda served the baked flounder, salad, broccoli and new potatoes with practiced ease.

Grant smiled graciously. Margaret had forgotten how good looking he was. Black curls fell in casual disarray about his brows. His strong jaw, high cheek bones indicated Indian ancestry. The white silk shirt billowed about his waist and disappeared into his black slacks. She understood why he was America's heart throb. He had a commanding aura about him Margaret thought.

He smiled as if he could read her thoughts. She hoped he couldn't.

"How's the flounder?" Grant repeated.

"What? I haven't tasted it," she confessed. He laughed.

~****~

**Chapter 9**

Margaret's expression was unreadable. Was he coming on to strong? Margaret had a faraway look in her eyes. She was striking in lavender Grant thought. Her violet eyes were electric. Finely attuned to her, Grant wanted to fulfill her needs. Couldn't she see that? A man couldn't expose his vulnerability. He had his reputation to consider.

Margaret snapped back to the present when laughter overcame him. He repeated the question. She remained silent. Was she sorry she came? He certainly was not.

Lifting a fork with fish to her mouth, Margaret savored the flounder. It was tender and tasty. "It's wonderful," she said with a smile.

"Catherine's flounder is exquisite," Grant said approvingly. White wine was served with the meal.

He offered a toast. "Here's to us."

She lifted her glass to his and nodded. He moved closer. Her pulse increased to double time. She started to move away.

"Margaret?" Grant lips trailed lightly along her neck. "What's wrong?"

"We should go into the study, I want to discuss my ideas for the house," Margaret remarked with calm reserve.

"I'd like to," he began, then he seemed to think better of it."Alright, after you." He rose.

Maintaining her distance she walked into the study. "I've reviewed your suggestions," Margaret managed. "They're good. What I have in mind will add a perk."

"Oh?"

"Yes. The house needs warmth."

"So do I."

"Stop fooling around."

"I'm serious." Grant gave a playful grin.

"You hired me to decorate your home," she reminded. "And not --"

"For services rendered," Grant completed the statement.

"We should reach an understanding."

"I thought we had. I'm the employer."

"And you call the shots!" Margaret said sardonically.

"So you *do* understand."

"Well understand this!" Margaret exclaimed, her voice rose an octave. "What happened last night, will not happen again," she explained. "I'm here to do a job and that's all!"

"Why are you angry?" Grant asked calmly.

"Why? I'll tell you why," she stammered.

He studied her with apparent curiosity. "Did I fail to please you?"

"Ah …"

"Do you feel desired?" Grant moved closer."Because you are. I protect what is mine."

"That's just --"

Before she could complete the statement, his mouth covered hers.

"Grant?" Margaret uttered between kisses.

"For once, relax. Follow your instincts," he coaxed.

Involuntarily her arms wrapped around his neck. Once again, Grant controlled the situation.

He lifted his head. "Decorate the house as if it belonged to you," Grant whispered."I trust you." His eyes met hers. "Trust me."

She could deny him nothing, when he looked at her this way.

"Trust you?" she considered it.

"Yes."

"That could be dangerous," Margaret said coquettishly.

"I hope so."

"What do you have in mind?"

"Oh let's see," he kissed her fingertips, lingering longer than necessary on each one. The sensation tantalized her senses.

It was unfair for one man to have such power over her. The ability to make her wish for more. A relationship between them was out of the question. He would never change.

"I don't want to rush you. I've enjoyed your company tonight. We'll discuss your plans to redecorate tomorrow morning. I wish to say goodnight," Grant said.

~****~

She woke early the next morning replaying last night's events in her mind. She was here to do a job. Remember that! Margaret's subconscious cried. A relationship between them would surely bring heart ache. There was no future in it.

A knock at the door interrupted her thoughts.

"Margaret?" Grant queried.

"Yes?"

"I'll meet you downstairs for breakfast."

"I'll be down in a few minutes," she replied.

Surprised he had stayed home, Margaret scrambled into her clothes. Were they any farther in understanding their relationship? Or had Grant managed a respite?

Today she would try the samples she had brought in the various rooms of the house. A perfectionist, Margaret wanted to create a distinctive mood in each room yet reflect the owner. She was pleased Grant would accompany her today and she planned to ask him several questions.

Breakfast was delightful with its appetizing choices. Grant was in the best of spirits today laughing and offering brilliant conversation. They began with the upstairs.

"Which do you think is better?" Margaret held a sample of wallpaper for his inspection, then another.

Furrowing his brows, Grant considered each intently.

She displayed fabric samples in the same manner. The two burgundy wing back chairs would compliment the splash of colors in the room. Thoughtfully he considered her suggestions.

"I like royal blue, burgundy, beige and brown with the yellow," Grant managed after careful deliberation.

He was pleasant company throughout the day as they went from room to room. Occasionally Margaret would discover his eyes on her, as she looked up from the samples. His attention would turn a girl's head she thought. If she allowed it!

Where had the day gone? He had been professional and thoroughly interested in the results. Margaret was pleased with his choices several times they echoed her own.

Grant observed her ostensible excitement of the renovations. His eyes would never tire of their feast on her.

Margaret was an intriguing, independent woman, full of surprises.

"I guess that wraps it up," Margaret said with a sigh. "I'll order the supplies tomorrow from New York."

His eyes were riveted on her. He moved forward, bringing his arms loosely around her. "Good. I can't wait to see them." Grant grinned devilishly.

"What?" Margaret began. "Does my slip show?"

He chuckled. "No. You're thorough, beautiful and enticing." He lowered his head.

She dodged. "Wait a minute. I think you've forgotten this is strictly business."

"Hardly. I've been a good boy all day," he reasoned. "It's recess."

"Grant you're asking for trouble. You know as well as I, this is temporary. Why complicate the matter?"

"Trouble is my middle name," he grinned seductively. "You heard me. It's bigger than both of us. Give up?" Again, he lowered his head and drew her near.

"Look this is all very flattering," Margaret offered in exasperation. "Please could we forget the whole romantic scene?"

"Like you said, I'm looking for trouble."

"This will not work," she scolded.

"Work wasn't what I had in mind." His gaze held hers.

"That's not fair," Margaret challenged.

"You're right," he whispered as he advanced on her.

"This scene is to perfect; to rehearsed." Margaret doubted that he listened. "I'm not interested."

"What troubles you?"

"Nothing."

"Why did you leave St. Raphael's without saying goodbye?"

"You lied to me," Margaret blurted.

"Oh, really?" Grant asked flabbergasted, his eyes widened. "I don't recall you mentioning a fiancée."

"You know about Phillip?"

"A small omission on your part. Come on, Margaret. I'm the one who should be angry."

"You … you?" she shrieked.

"I never claimed, I told the *whole* truth," he admitted. "At least, I'm not engaged." His eyes narrowed as he lowered them to hers.

"That's putting it mildly," she retorted. For a extended moment each glared at the other.

Simultaneously they burst into laughter.

"I apologize for my dishonesty," Grant offered. "I wanted you to like me for myself. Not because I'm Grant Michaels the actor."

"The gigolo," Margaret added nervously.

"In the past that may have been true." Grant stepped forward, resting his large hands on her shoulders. "The only thing I lied about was my work. The rest is true."

"Really?"

"Of course." He nodded. "What about Phillip?"

"I called off the engagement. Phillip's a friend." A familiar warmness washed over her. "I saw your picture with Nina Albright," she ventured in an attempt to clear the air.

"That was for publicity," Grant remarked. "My name's constantly linked with a woman. My image, you know. Again, its publicity."

"You're convincing," Margaret muttered through hooded eyes.

What caused her to sway? She felt light on her feet.

"I am an actor," Grant whispered. "Let's see, where were we?" He drew her into his embrace.

Margaret's senses reeled.

"I've missed you. You drive me mad with need," he uttered while he rained kisses along the column of her neck. Erotically he bit the lobe of her ear, his tongue slipped inside.

Why did he lose control with this woman?

Startled by a shrill ringing sound, he turned. Grant felt as though everything moved in slow motion. Her lips were inviting. His head dipped.

Absently Margaret lifted her gaze and swallowed a lump in her throat. Hilda was standing behind him.

"I beg your pardon, sir," Hilda began. "You have an urgent call."

Grant muttered an expletive under his breath. Summoning his control, he turned.

"Thank you, Hilda."

Embarrassed, Margaret made a polite excuse and left the room. Hilda followed, closing the study doors behind them. Margaret continued to move upstairs.

"Hello?" Grant growled.

"Hey, buddy."

"Bill -!" he barked.

"Wait a minute!" Bill cautioned. "I take it, I've interrupted something important?"

"Get on with it. You said it was urgent."

"The wife and I are having a party tonight for the crew," Bill began.

"Yeah?"

"Of all people to drop by unexpectedly," Bill groaned. "John Harris, the producer is here with his entourage."

"What has that to do with me?" Grant pushed a hand through his hair impatiently.

"He plans to back out on the film. I think you'd better come over, pronto."

"I'm leaving now." He dropped the phone in its cradle. "Dammit!" Grant glimpsed the time, nine o'clock in the evening.

He took the stairs two at a time and rapped on Margaret's door.

"Yes?"

"Open the door." The tone of his voice indicated he was disturbed.

Margaret opened the door. "What's wrong?"

"I have a problem. It concerns my work," Grant explained taking her hand. "Come with me."

"Where are you taking me?"

"To a party. I realize it's short notice, but it's important."

"But I am not dressed."

"You're beautiful," he interjected. "You'll do me proud." The mischievous gleam in his eyes returned.

"Give me a moment. I'll be right with you." Margaret applied fresh lipstick while she studied her reflection.

Moments later Grant informed Hilda of their plans. Outside, the chauffeur held open the door to the beige Rolls-Royce. Were it not for the constant reminder of his extravagant lifestyle, Margaret would consider him like anyone else.

The automobile moved easily along the hilly countryside. The ride was unlike any Margaret had experienced. Although it was Saturday night, the automobile effectively muffled the sounds outside. The trip over was made in uncomfortable silence. Margaret tried to bridge it with strained conversation to no avail.

Why had he asked her along? she wondered.

The chauffeur guided the grand automobile into a prominent neighborhood, making several turns before entering a long, circular drive. A single story stone house with huge double doors came into view. The house was typically Californian in appearance. Alight with music emanating from it. No doubt there was a party in progress Margaret thought.

Grant grasped Margaret's elbow as they approached the entrance.

"Hey, Grant's here," a voice called from the crowd.

"It's about time," chimed another.

"And he's as gorgeous as ever," a sultry female offered.

Smiling, Grant made polite salutations as he pushed through the crowd. He seemed determined to find someone.

A medium-height, sandy-haired man approached. The tension between both men was almost palpable.

"He's with Emily on the patio," the man said hurriedly. It was apparent that he was making a concerted effort to calm down, he smiled. "You must be Margaret?"

Puzzled she glanced in Grant's direction.

"Bill Wallace, Grant's best friend and advisor." He offered his hand.

"Margaret Stewart," she responded, taking his hand lightly.

"Pleased to meet you," Bill said, male appreciation apparent in his eyes.

"An unexpected pleasure," Margaret managed.

"You devil," Bill scolded mockingly, as he punched Grant's arm. "Trying to keep her to yourself, huh?"

Grant pretended to retaliate. Both men chuckled.

"Champagne?" Bill offered.

"How lovely," Margaret replied. Grant nodded. Bill gestured with a wave of his hand to a waitress carrying a tray of drinks.

"Two please," Bill requested, accepting the glasses of bubbly from her.

After a whirlwind day, Margaret thought she deserved it. Perhaps the drink would slow her bounding pulse. Lifting her glass, Margaret took a sip. The bubbles tickled her nose. Grant downed his drink and asked for another. Bill whispered in his ear. With an upward turn of his hand, Bill turned to walk away. "Will you excuse me, Margaret?"

"Please by my guest."

Grant leaned closer to her ear. "Bill's wife, Emily will be over in a moment. She'll show you around. I need to speak with Bill and the producer in private."

"No problem. Go ahead." Margaret flashed her best smile. He released a deep sigh.

"I won't be long. I promise." He turned and walked away. Although he returned her smile, Margaret knew his agitation was barely restrained.

Margaret's gaze traveled the room. Groups of two or three were either engaged in dance or stood around the large buffet table. The music was a collage of soft fifties-to-sixties jazz with an occasional Sinatra tune drifting throughout the house.

Someone tapped her shoulder. Margaret spun around.

"Hello, Margaret, I'm Emily," the petite raven-haired woman said. "We're pleased you could come.

"How kind, Emily," she replied. "What a lovely party."

"The truth is, it began small," Emily sighed."Word travels fast as you can see. Have you tried the buffet?"

"We had dinner before coming."

"Come I'll introduce you to our friends," Emily said, taking her hand."The men could be tied up for hours."

Margaret glanced over her shoulder to the patio. Grant appeared intent in conversation, as he gestured with his hands. He didn't look happy.

She feigned interest in the lengthy introductions and followed Emily through the crowd. This looks like the Los Angeles freeway at rush hour, she thought, with wall-to-wall people. She took a glass of champagne from a passing waitress.

Clearly proud of her home Emily gave Margaret a tour of it. "I've heard so much about you," Emily commented with a broad smile.

"From who?"

"Bill." Emily sharply inclined her head, a saucy grin on her face."You're Grant's mystery woman."

"I've been called many things, but never --"

"Since his return from the Caribbean, he hasn't been the same," Emily interrupted. "He's been a hermit. Hardly the former Hollywood playboy who used to be the life of the party."

"He's changed?"

"Drastically. So you see?"

"Afraid not."

"Bill said it's because of you. We've wanted to meet you for some time," Emily explained. "Our boy's smitten."

Margaret's heart swelled. Could Grant be in love with her? The thought seemed to unbelievable to entertain. Regardless she fell victim to the silly assumption. It served her right she told herself he never told her he loved her.

"Men like Grant belong to their public," Margaret replied. "Women fall over themselves to get to him. It's just to easy."

"That's why we're surprised. How are you finding Hollywood?"

"Fast paced like New York."

"I think you'll enjoy living in Hollywood."

"I'm not sure I understand," Margaret said, puzzled.

"You'll want to be near Grant," Emily said matter-of-factly.

"You've been misinformed. Grant hired me to redecorate his home. Afterward, I plan to return to New York."

"I'm sorry. I didn't mean to pry."

"No? Then, what?" Grant asked with an impish grin.

"Oh nothing, just girl talk," Margaret dismissed.

"Excuse me, I see Madeline. Nice meeting you Margaret." Emily moved in the direction of an older guest, motioning to her.

"Did you take care of the problem?" Margaret questioned.

"It took some negotiating, but yes. Has Emily kept you properly entertained?"

"She's nice and fond of you."

"Can you blame her?" He kissed her neck.

"You're not short of conceit."

"Miss me?"

"Maybe a little," she replied in a sassy tone.

"You owe me a dance."

"I pay my debts." Margaret moved into his arms.

"Bill thinks you're a real looker," Grant said softly."I told him you were spoken for."

"How so?"

"You're with me."

She knew their relationship was temporary at best and prided herself as being a realist. But tonight she would give into the fantasy and live for the moment. And think about this tomorrow.

Margaret buried her face in his chest as he pulled her closer than necessary.

~****~

**Chapter 10**

"The project in Bel-Air must be some assignment," Debra mused.

"It is," Margaret agreed. "I'll need the supplies as soon as possible from the manufacturer. I am anxious to begin."

"I'll get right on it," Debra answered. "It may take two or three days to fill a large order. I'll do my best."

"How's business?" queried Margaret.

"Sean's filling in nicely," her secretary replied. "How long will you be away?"

"His Bel-Air home is large. Perhaps a month or two. I dislike being away so long."

"If there's a problem, call me," Debra responded. "We'll take care of everything." When Margaret remained silent.

"Besides, think of the great press. The phone will ring off the wall."

"You're an angel," Margaret said sincerely.

Debra rang off. She hoped she hadn't forgotten anything Margaret thought, replacing the receiver. Uncertainty filled her as to why she'd been fortuitous to land the job, but Margaret was grateful. This assignment could make *Unicorn Designs*. Debra was right, the press would be invaluable. Her mind buzzed with the possibilities.

Her knowledge of the owner would make the job easier. Margaret had several ideas and she began to jot them down. Grant's house was one of her larger assignments. He had given her an unlimited budget. Her talents were free to coordinate the artwork, color, fabric, drapes and shades in each room.

Margaret was accustomed to working within a budget. Sometimes she'd had to stretch a dollar or two. Nevertheless, this was not the case. The monetary consideration here could be astounding.

Grant gave her the parlor as an office. Making herself at home, she threw samples askew. When Margaret worked she was oblivious to neatness. She considered herself an artist and was given to periods of being temperamental. She consulted the yellow pages for upholsterers, painters, paper hanger and carpenters. Experience taught her it took time to find the right people. She took pride in her work and demanded nothing less of her fellow workers.

She remembered last night with delightful reflection. They danced until midnight and returned to the Bel-Air mansion. He bewildered her when he kissed her and turned on his heel to leave. The man was unpredictable.

~****~

"Hey buddy," Bill was at Grant's side. No doubt Margaret was a good influence Bill thought. Grant looked content. If this woman was the key to his happiness, so be it. The ill-tempered man who left for the Caribbean was a real pain in the back side.

The previous three or four months Bill had considered resigning as Grant's financial advisor. The man had become onerous. Bill knew that somewhere along the way a gasket would blow. He didn't want to be around when it happened. But times, like people, change.

"The scene's not convincing, Grant," the director emphasized."Let's break for lunch. Everyone return in one hour -- on time!"

The crew dispersed, each muttering under their breath. It had been a full day with the director pushing hard since five-thirty. Grant was sure the director had awaken mad at the world. He refused to let anything ruin his mood.

"Let me take you to lunch?" Bill asked.

"Let's hit it." Grant pushed up from his seat.

"Where would you like to go?"

"Anywhere away from here," Grant added.

Bill drove to a small Italian restaurant nearby without careening into anyone. Small miracle Grant thought the man was the world's worst driver. Made him nervous as hell.

"Thanks for coming over last night," Bill said after the waitress left with their order.

"Saved our lives," Grant laughed.

"The old bear was set on backing out," Bill remarked jokingly."Wish I'd taped the whole thing. You were great."

"One must be cognizant of the opponent's weakness," Grant began. "And he owes me one."

The waitress returned moments later with two bottles of Perrier and glasses, turned then departed.

"Margaret is one helluva woman. Ou-la-la! You're one lucky son-of-a-gun."

"Thanks, pal." Grant poured the carbonated water into his glass.

"Emily likes her too. Although …" Bill was usually the boisterous kind, he hesitated. Grant sensed trouble. This was unlike Bill.

"But what?" Grant began. When Bill paused, he said, "Let's have it."

"It's none of my business."

"You just made it your business."

"Well, Emily spoke with Margaret and it seems she doesn't plan to stay. Margaret claims you're friends. I thought you'd like to know."

"Friends, huh?"

"How are things really between you?"

"Friends?" Grant repeated in dismay.

"Something wrong with your hearing?"

"I'll make her think friends," Grant said more to himself.

"How can she resist the charms of Grant Michaels?" Bill hazarded. "I don't believe it. That's a first." Bill recognized the thoughtful look. Grant was plotting something.

~****~

Margaret narrowed her choices for workers by mid-afternoon. Stretching, she rose from the desk. When she worked Margaret wore faded jeans and an old cotton blouse. She appeared a waif instead of the successful business woman, she was. Margaret was determined to look the house over once to make sure she hadn't overlooked anything.

Afternoon became evening and she sank into a chair. Errant strands of hair hung in her face, she pushed them off her face. Sighing, she knew Grant's home would be a task. Margaret loved challenges.

"Well, now. What do we have here?" Grant greeted from the doorway.

She looked over her shoulder. Darn! She meant to bathe and change before he arrived. She looked like an orphan Margaret thought.

He walked into the parlor, a broad smile on his face. I've completed most of the preliminary work," she defended as Grant continued to stare mutely at her. "I know. I look like a waif."

"A beautiful waif," he corrected.

Self consciously, she made an attempt to straighten her hair knotted on top of her head. It's useless Margaret thought and gave up the fruitless endeavor. Truth was she had been in the basement and other dirty places. She was a complete wreck.

"You bet, and I'm the Queen of Sheba," Margaret drawled. When she was nervous, she would make jokes or feign disinterest.

He threw his head back and laughed heartily. "And a cynic."

Ignoring his response, she forged ahead, "You're home early!" She hadn't meant for it to sound an accusation.

"I do live here."

"I'm surprised, that's all."

"We began earlier today. Finally the director was merciful." Why did he feel the need to explain his arrival? It wasn't as though he had committed a crime. Women!

He moved closer. Planning to dart out of the room, she stood. A sudden wave of warmness washed over him. He wanted to protect her, always. Somehow, she looked more endearing.

"Would you like to go out tonight?" Grant asked softly. Her brows creased, she tilted her head."I thought we could have dinner and I'll show you the town?"

"Sounds good. I'll need thirty or forty minutes to bathe and dress," Margaret replied.

"Great. Now, run along." He swatted her bottom as she turned to leave. Surprised, she jumped, releasing a sharp gasp from her throat.

Grant busied himself with making telephone calls. Minutes later he bounded the stairs for a quick shower and change.

The water pelted from the shower head, relieving his tension. A bath would restore him. "Ow!" he groaned, trying to rinse the soap from of his eyes. He could feel every nerve come alive as the warm water pelted his skin.

Stepping from the shower, Grant dried himself and slung a towel low on his hips. He wiped the foggy mirror with another towel, and began to lather his face. A shave would rid him of the dark stubble that accumulated. He wanted the night to be perfect.

Her uneasiness when he arrived had been more than apparent. She quickly pushed an impatient hand through her tousled hair. Grant couldn't remember when Margaret had looked better. In fact, she looked vulnerable.

Margaret studied her reflection in the full length mirror. She washed her hair doubting he would relish a date who smelled of sweat, dust and spider webs. Her moist hair pulled into a ponytail, braided and coiled at her nape, lent a regal appearance. Smiling she considered she looked similar to a medieval princess.

As she descended the last step, Margaret saw Grant issuing instructions to a servant. Her heartbeat grew rapid.

The impeccable fit of his tailored navy blue suit showcased an athletic physique. He turned, as a slow smile spread on his face. He extended a hand to her. A low wolf whistle escaped his lips."You're fortunate, we're going out." He shook his head slightly as mischief danced in his eyes, he moved a hand to her low back.

"I'm glad you like it." Margaret shot him a side long glance over her shoulder.

Outside the door a burgundy Jaguar XJS convertible awaited.

"Where's the chauffeur?" she teased as he opened her door.

"I gave him the night off. I'll drive." Grant climbed behind the wheel."Any objections?"

She laughed."Do you know how to drive this?"

He scowled and shifted gears.

Her seat belt fastened, Margaret just leaned back when the car abruptly lurched forward with its tires screeching.

"Take it easy," Margaret shrieked."I prefer to remain in one piece."

No response followed. The automobile gained in speed.

The cool breeze that blew through her hair felt almost sinful. A half moon lit the starry night as the car moved through traffic.

"Where are we going?" Margaret queried.

"It's a surprise," Grant interrupted, changing lanes in traffic. He swore as another driver moved in front of them without signaling. The car swerved. Margaret bit her lower lip. "How's it coming?"

"I beg your pardon?"

"The renovation."

"Oh, that. I thought you referred to my heart lodged in my throat. That man's crazy." Her gaze followed the speeding car that whizzed past from nowhere."Well, I've done a lot of the ground work and ordered supplies. Debra will fill the order as soon as possible. Today I checked the basement. It needs work."

"Take all the time you need," he encouraged.

"I have a schedule to maintain," she warned stiffly. "And a business waiting for me in New York." Margaret shifted her gaze to the passenger window otherwise she might have seen him roll his eyes.

Much later he stopped in front of *Mann's Chinese Theater.* A valet opened the door, Margaret stepped out. Grant was at her side within moments.

Inside they were shown to a reserved table.

"Good evening, Mr. Michaels," a man called from a nearby table. Grant nodded politely.

"I never expected anything so Hollywood," Margaret's voice trailed off as her gaze scanned the famous restaurant and club. A pulsing, jazzy tune filled the air.

"Does it meet your expectations?" he smiled, satisfied with himself.

"Definitely. I would like to see the imprints of the stars," Margaret said enthusiastically.

"You shall. In the old days it was called *Grauman's Chinese Theater.*

The food was exquisite. Grant showed her the famous impressions of the movie stars. Dismayed she noticed a slate that caught her eye, hand prints with the name, Grant Michaels scrawled haphazardly across the top.

"You never mentioned this," she said as she pointed to the slate with his handprints.

He gave an unconcerned groan. Grant grasped her hand. "Since you're properly in awe, I think we had better head for Malibu Beach. Ready?"

"What's in Malibu," she asked allowing him to usher her from the restaurant.

"I'll tell you about it in the car."

The burgundy convertible was promptly brought to the entrance. Once behind the wheel, Grant pulled into traffic and started for coastal route 101.

"It's twenty-five miles northwest of Los Angeles," Grant stated.

"Again, why Malibu?"

"*Tirage Studios'* owner, Jim Mc Kay is throwing a bash at his home. I have to attend. You understand? Public relations," he explained.

"You don't believe in giving much notice do you?" she chided mockingly.

"I just found out this afternoon," Grant reasoned. "Do you mind?"

The cool California night air refreshed Margaret as the automobile easily took the curves along the coastal highway. Moonlight reflected softly off the Pacific Ocean.

Grant had gone lengths to plan a romantic evening without mentioning a word. His savoir faire invigorated Margaret. He was vibrant, aristocratic, charismatic – the American woman's dream. He was every woman's dream.

He must have felt her eyes on him, Grant turned his head slightly and smiled. Margaret trembled. Misunderstanding her action, Grant motioned for her to move into the cradle of his arm. She moved closer. He secured her with a light squeeze.

A series of turns brought them into a private upscale neighborhood. Each house or estate covered three or four large lots. Grant stopped before a large gate that guarded the entrance. A white stucco wall surrounded the property like a fortress.

He spoke into a small black box perched on the left side of the gate, "Grant Michaels."A moment later the gate opened to allow entry then closed quietly behind them. A uniformed man inside a small guard house gave a half salute as they passed. Grant waved.

The long drive was surrounded on each side by a well manicured landscape, undulating hills and illuminated by a shower of lights arranged in key spots to accentuate the landscape.

Ahead a magnificent white stucco mansion was perched like a proud bird on a hill. Four large columns supported a roof that jutted over the entryway. Margaret saw valets parking and retrieving vehicles against the roar of the ocean surf.

Grant lifted a brass ring on the immense walnut doors and knocked. Moments later they were greeted by a butler and shown where the others were.

They stepped down into an enormous ballroom with several French doors displaying a panoramic view of the Pacific

Ocean. A gentle wind blew inside carrying in its wake the rhythmic sound of the waves lapping the shore. A quartet played a romantic, jazzy tune. The sultry female vocalist sang something about, 'silent touches, meaningful touches.' The words captured Margaret's attention.

~****~

Chapter 11

Grant continued through the crowd with Margaret in tow, stopping when they reached the dance floor to take her in his arms. Perhaps the lyrics titillated him as they held her.

"Happy?" he whispered as he placed a light kiss to her nape. Lifting his head he rested his forehead against hers.

"I don't know of a woman who would complain. But then, you know this," Margaret said softly, a satisfied gleam in her eyes. He gave a helpless shrug of his shoulders.

"You're the loveliest woman here," he uttered huskily. His gaze travelled to the scintillating, black dress that skimmed seductively off her shoulders.

He planned the ideal seduction scene. The problem was, it worked Margaret thought. Initially she tried to avoid his attentions. Grant played the scene so many times he had it down to a science. Margaret was convinced he must be a warlock. Most men searched their whole lives for the attributes most women found attractive. Grant had it all.

Grant's electric eyes darkened to obsidian when filled with desire as now. His magnetic touch sent pulsing waves along her nerves she considered wistfully.

Someone tapped Grant's shoulder but he ignored them pulling her closer yet. One song ended, without delay, another began. Still they danced to the collage of music. She hadn't missed the several admiring female glances Grant drew effortlessly.

"What's the occasion?" Margaret asked as she withdrew slightly, her gaze met his.

"The Hollywood crowd parties a lot. We work hard and play hard."

"This could turn a girl's head." She lifted a hand, gesturing the entire atmosphere.

"Impressed?"

"Yes. Do you live this way?"

"Partying?"

"Of course," Margaret began."Do you ever tire of the limelight?"

"Yes," he answered flatly.

"I didn't mean to offend you. Please don't misunderstand."

A rock tune began.

"What?" He cupped his ear. Her lips moved but he couldn't make out the words. Grant motioned for them to step outside. She followed suit.

A silver-haired man stopped Grant as they started for the patio, whispering something in Grant's ear. When Grant did the same, both smiled impishly. The older man slapped Grant's back, then turned and walked away.

Outside they could hear the music distinctly, in any event at least they could converse.

"Who's the older man?"

"Jim Mc Kay, the owner of the studio. He wished me luck with the beautiful young lady," Grant explained with a wicked grin.

"I hope he's not offended we left?"

"He was young once," Grant said as he nudged Margaret down the steep stairs made of stone to the beach below.

"We haven't been here long. Everyone will think we're rude," Margaret insisted.

"The parties are all the same."

"Why did you come?"

"It's expected of me," Grant said more to himself. "I knew, I would enjoy it if you came with me."

She leaned to slip off her high heels. Déjà Veau he thought.

"Margaret what do you think of California?"

"It's bustling and beautiful."

"I'd like to you to meet my family," Grant said as they strolled along the shore."What do you say?"

"I would love to," she said approvingly.

He turned to face her. Gently cupping her face with both hands, he lowered his head. His kiss was filled with tender desperation and promise that consumed Margaret.

~****~

Excited by the possibilities, Margaret worked to organize her thoughts. She didn't want to leave out a single detail. She would make this her best work.

Hearing footsteps, she looked up.

"Miss Stewart," Hilda began."A truck delivered several boxes for you."

"Hallelujah!" She rose. "Where?"

"They're in the foyer."

"Hilda you've made me the happiest woman," Margaret said moving an arm around the servant's shoulders as they walked from the room. She giggled at Hilda's puzzled expression.

"You would think they were gold," Hilda commented sardonically.

"Much better than that. It's like Christmas."

Margaret couldn't wait to unpack the contents and begin work. Hilda and Catherine helped Margaret carry the boxes into the parlor.

"If you need anything child, just give us a call," Catherine said as the women left Margaret to her work.

"I will thanks." Margaret glanced at her watch, eleven o'clock. Margaret busied herself to the task at hand. She would open the boxes, and contact the workers to begin tomorrow. Two weeks had passed since her arrival in California and she was anxious to begin.

Two hours later and the last box opened she commended Debra on a job well done. She would give her secretary a raise when she returned to New York.

By two o'clock the next day Margaret completed her calls. Completing the sketches and separating the supplies into the respective rooms would take the remainder of the day. The work would commence tomorrow. She switched the stereo to a classical station. The soothing music would promote creativity.

Catherine served lunch in the parlor when Margaret did not offer to budge. The cook fussed and chattered on, asking, "Do you want to say skinny? You need some meat on your bones." Given this, Catherine turned and left.

Later that evening Margaret yawned and rose from her desk. She noticed it was seven o'clock.

Hilda knocked on the parlor door and entered.

"I forgot the time. Is dinner ready?" Margaret offered.

"Yes, miss. Mr. Michaels will not be joining us for dinner. He's been detained at work."

"I see."

"Will you dine in the formal dining room, Miss Stewart?"

"No. Ask Catherine to prepare a sandwich for me. I'll have it upstairs. I'm tired but I still have work to complete."

"Very good, Miss." Hilda left the room.

Margaret felt a pang of disappointment. She hadn't realized how much she looked forward to his arrival. She collected her sketch pad and notes, then crossed the room, closing the door quietly behind her.

The hot rose scented bubble bath titillated her skin. She leaned back against the tub, closing her eyes.

~****~

The late September evening was cool. The director insisted on several takes of a scene Grant felt was performed correctly the first time. But what did he know?

Unlike some Hollywood starlets, it was a pleasure to work with Nina Albright. She had a right to an enormous ego he thought. Any man would give his right arm to be cast with her.

The love scene was beginning to get under his skin. Hell, he liked Nina respected her even but to kiss her thirty takes well, this was asking too much. Ordinarily he enjoyed his work oblivious to the time. Lately, he couldn't wait to get home.

He hired Margaret to redecorate his home thinking perhaps he would see she wasn't special thereby he would get her out of his system. It was just a phase he told himself. Grant was surprised to learn he wanted to see more of her.

Nine o'clock rolled around with the director pleased at last. It was a good thing Grant mused because his lips were chapped. During the drive home, Grant replayed the telephone conversation with Anna earlier.

"How's it going, little brother?" Anna drawled.

"Great with the exception of the director. Would you like to help me drown him?" Grant chuckled at the prospect.

"I saw mom and dad today. They asked about you." Anna's voice held a trace of irritation.

"That's why I called," Grant explained. "I want them to meet Margaret."

"She's here in California?" queried Anna in disbelief.

"Yes." Grant smiled to himself.

"I don't believe it! You were so touchy before when the subject of Margaret came up. When do you plan to do this?"

"Saturday is their anniversary. Let's call the family together. Have dinner catered at their place? I'll bring Margaret."

"That's wonderful. Leave the details to me. You can foot the bill." Enthusiasm laced her voice. "Sevenish?"

"See you then." He pulled the Jaguar into the drive at his Bel-Air home and hopped out. The chauffeur met him, climbed inside, then drove the grand automobile into the garage.

Grant couldn't wait to tell Margaret about the plans for Saturday. He hoped she was still awake.

Hilda met him at the door with Catherine at her heel. Both women were a second or third mother to him and spoiled him terribly. Apparently each had something urgent to discuss with him. The sprinkler system was in need of repair. A large shopping bill had arrived today and Catherine hadn't purchase all that – it must be a mistake. The water pipes in one of the bathrooms made noise. In addition, something had to be done about the gardener!

"Whoa!" Grant bought his hands together to form a 'T.' "Timeout!"

Flabbergasted both women stopped in mid-sentence.

"Have you eaten Mr. Michaels?" Catherine asked sheepishly.

"Yes, at the studio. Listen, it has been a long day. Make a list and we'll see to the details tomorrow. All I want is a hot bath."

"But --" Hilda began.

"Goodnight," Grant interrupted. He quickly mounted the stairs. He could see the lights under Margaret's door as he passed. He'd speak with her after he bathed.

Thirty minutes later he opened his door and walked out. The house was silent and dimly lit. Everyone had gone to bed. The light remained under Margaret's door. His knuckles contacted it.

Moments later the door swung open.

"Who?" She gasped when she almost collided with him. "Grant, it's late." Margaret cinched her robe tighter about her waist. Anxiously, she pushed at the back of her hair. She had been reading in bed.

"May I come in?"

She heaved a sigh and narrowed her eyes. "That's not a good idea.

"Why?"

"People may get the wrong impression."

"I need to speak with you," he pressed.

"Ten minutes, tops!" Margaret warned. His incongruous grin annoyed her.

"Sure," Grant said calmly as he stepped inside, closing the door behind him."Remember I mentioned, I'd like you to meet my family?"

"Yes?" Margaret asked suspiciously.

"Saturday is their anniversary. My sisters and I planned a family gathering at their home. Anna's taking care of the details and the catering," Grant explained. "Go with me?"

"I'd love to."

"That was almost too easy."

"If you prefer, I could hold out longer? Make you work for it," Margaret challenged with a limpid look.

"That won't be necessary." He leaned back in the chair his legs crossed at the ankles, his hands laced behind his head.

"Don't make yourself to comfortable," she reminded. "You're not staying."

"What are you afraid of?" he taunted.

"Nothing." She took a seat on the bedside.

"Oh, really?" He wasn't convinced.

No response followed.

"You're afraid of me. Why?"

She was afraid of herself Margaret wanted to shout.

She shook her head.

"Prove it," Grant challenged."Come here."

"You were just leaving," she supplied in an effort to thwart his challenge.

"We're not strangers by far."

"I know your prowess in the seduction department but you've worn them thin."

"You think I like to play games?"

"Don't you?" Margaret countered.

"What gave you that impression?"

"You can be anyone. Convince anyone."

He made a steeple with his hands. "It's called acting. I do it for a living."

"Unfortunately you let it carry over into reality," Margaret said sternly.

"You don't really believe that?"

"You're to smooth, Grant."

"What the hell is that supposed to mean?"

"Actors are actors because they enjoy being other people and in other situations.

He shot her a bewildered look.

"You're the man every girl dreams of, hopes for, and fantasizes about. But -" She glanced down at her feet.

"But not you," Grant finished. He rose and in three strides stood before her. Convulsively gripping her shoulders in his large hands he demanded, "Look at me!"

Margaret gazed up mutely.

"What is it you find so objectionable about me?" His eyes blazed white heat.

"I've never denied the physical attraction," she said scarcely more than a whisper.

"So that's it?" He ran a hand through his moist hair. Grant swore. "There sure as hell is!"

She remained silent.

"Say something. Damn it!" He gave her a slight shake.

"I won't be at your beckon call," Margaret shot back angrily.

"What?"

"I'm not one of your possessions," she snapped.

Summoning all his self-restraint, Grant inhaled deeply before he sat beside her on the bed. His voice lowered a few octaves, he began, "Margaret, I do respect you. I could never be oblivious of your feelings."

"I know you mean well. It's just …"

Grant kissed her nape and stroked her hair. "Just what?"

"I can't think when you do that."

"Go on." He rained kisses along her jaw and neck.

"You don't play fair," she pouted.

"Honey, there's nothing fair about love and war." He grinned, lifting her chin.

His kiss filled her senses.

"But-"

Grant shifted, pushing her back on the bed. "Hush, Margaret. Love me."

Slowly her rigid posture relaxed as Grant covered her body with his. Her robe opened, displaying her softly curved breasts with the outline of her nipples apparent beneath the satin fabric.

He knew she had doubts and fears. He wanted to show her how much he had grown to care for her. This was the only way he knew to communicate his feelings. Damn right there's a physical attraction he thought. He had awakened several times with a pulsing heat in his loins just thinking about her.

Margaret's hands moved eagerly over his body. He trembled as her hand slid to his groin. She could feel the heat of his blatant arousal beneath his jeans.

"Oh, baby ... that's it."

Margaret reveled in the heady sense of power she had over him. Apparently Grant was as easily affected by her touch. She pushed him onto his back, meshing her fingers with his, above his head. His hooded eyes played havoc with her heart.

He lifted his head, capturing a nipple in his mouth. The satin became wet.

"Oh, yes" she moaned as she ground her hips against his. He arched into her. His breathing was shallow, Grant lifted her gown to her waist, slipping his hands inside her panties.

"Margaret," he groaned."Tell me what you want." He cupped her bottom.

She moved his hand to the apex of her femininity. Margaret urged, "You, here." She writhed against him. He shifted to his side.

"No, don't," she uttered.

"I'm not leaving baby." Frantically he worked to unfasten his jeans. "I couldn't even if I wanted to. I can bear it no longer. I've got to have you."

He managed the last button and lifted his hips as Margaret tugged off his jeans.

Before she lowered herself, he said, "Wait." Puzzled, she hesitated. He raised her gown over her head. Margaret wiggled out of her panties.

"Now. Come here." He leaned back on the bed, arms extended invitingly. She smiled devilishly and paused.

"Come here, baby. I ache for you."

She straddled his hips. He trembled as Margaret enfolded him. She did not move at first but she could feel him pulsate inside her. He arched his back. Slowly she began to move.

Feverishly the rhythm increased to a crescendo.

"Grant, now. Now!

He rolled to his side, taking her with him, legs intertwined, in one swift motion. Grant's mouth covered hers. His thrusts increased. A short time later, sated he held her close as both returned to earth once more.

Moments later he whispered, "Margaret could you be happy in California?" he asked.

"Yes. But my business is in New York."

Nothing ventured, nothing gained he thought.

"But could you imagine living in California?" Grant persisted.

"Don't be silly. My family and my life are in New York."

This was a switch, Grant mused. Ordinarily he was the one who remained cool and calm. Damn it, wasn't he a part of her life he wondered? An important part? Do you love me, Margaret? he wanted to ask. Bewildered and annoyed with her, he pushed up, then slipped into his jeans. He threw on his shirt and made for the door.

"Leaving?"

"Damn right!" The door closed firmly behind him.

If that doesn't beat all Margaret mused. Not even a thank you. Margaret was convinced he could turn his moods off and on like hot and cold water – a machine. She stomped the floor with one foot and began to pace. Margaret couldn't wait to return to New York. Actors are a lost cause, especially the dangerous Grant Michaels she considered.

~****~

**Chapter 12**

"Do you plan to return to New York? Or travel around endlessly?" Elisia chided.

"Mother I am not on vacation. I'm decorating Grant Michaels Bel-Air home.

"Why didn't you say so?" Elisia gushed. "Does he look as good in person as on the screen?"

"Better."

"What?"

"He looks better in person," Margaret teased.

"You were always the luckiest girl. Even when you were a child, the boys wouldn't leave you alone. Now, you're with the sexiest, most eligible bachelor in the country. What am I saying? The world."

"Take it easy, mother."

"I'll have to visit my little girl."

"Don't you dare!"

"Do you plan to keep him to yourself?"

"Mother!"

Margaret could hear her father's voice in the background.

"Kitten, how are you?" Brian Stewart greeted.

"Fine, Daddy. I miss both of you. How's Popcorn?"

"He's beginning to think he lives here," Brian chuckled. "Don't want a neurotic cat on your hands, do you?"

"Popcorn thinks he's human. I've noticed he likes to sleep on his back with his paws in the air and his head tilted sideways. He's a lot of things but neurotic isn't one of them." She laughed.

Brian Stewart joined in the laughter. "Alright, I'll give the phone to your mother. Bye, baby. Come home soon."

"I will daddy. Bye."

"It's time we had a chance to finish our conversation," Elisia fussed.

"Mother I would like to talk longer, but I have to go. I'll call again soon. Love to you and dad."

"We love you, too. Goodbye."

~****~

It was Wednesday and Margaret planned to make every moment count. The workers began today. The house buzzed with noise and the smell of fresh paint wafted in the air.

Catherine prepared sandwiches for the workers. She instructed each one to wipe their feet before entering certain areas of the house. The priceless crystal, figurines and artwork, Catherine informed were off limits.

The next two days Grant left before she awoke and he did not return until after she retired. Margaret knew he meant to avoid her. Who could figure the man? He'd had his way with her, now he would move on to new conquests.

The furniture had to be moved and covered. She tried to confine her efforts in two or three rooms at a time. Dressed in her reliable jeans and favorite work shirt, Margaret tied a scarf over her hair to protect it from paint and dust. Margaret was in her element instructing workers where to begin and when to be cautious. She stayed so busy that Catherine had to remind her to eat.

"You're gonna shrivel up and blow away," Catherine coaxed.

Occasionally Margaret would focus on Grant and the impasse they had reached -- so be it. She knew better than to become involved with him. But Grant's commanding aura refused to be taken lightly.

By Friday she missed him dreadfully. She had dressed to please him and it would be good to see him tonight. As she thought more and more of Saturday, she discovered she looked forward to meeting his family. Margaret hoped he hadn't cause to regret the invitation. She knew he was avoiding her.

Hilda informed her Grant would join her for dinner promptly at six-thirty. Tonight she would find out what troubled him. Deliberately she was a few minutes late to dinner. She didn't want to appear anxious. True to Hilda's word, Grant was seated at the dinner table when Margaret entered the dining room. He stood and inclined his head.

"Hello, Grant." Margaret flashed her best smile, exposing perfect teeth.

"Good evening," he returned. Seemingly Grant was a polite stranger.

"How are you?" queried Margaret as he pulled her chair back.

"Weary. It's been a hard week." In more ways than one he thought.

"It's good to see you," she offered pleasantly.

"How kind."

Classical music played softly in the background. Hilda served dinner by candlelight, then departed.

"What's the occasion?" Grant asked puzzled.

"I had nothing to do with this," Margaret chuckled. She made a sweeping gesture with her hand."We've been setup."

"Who? Never mind that, now." He grinned."Catherine."

"Yes, with Hilda's help."

"I'm sorry. They mean well," he muttered.

"No need to apologize. They're sweet. Both care a great deal for you."

"I'm a lucky man."

"Indeed."

The baked chicken and rice, tossed salad and mixed vegetables were delicious. The dessert was chocolate mousse, followed by coffee on the patio.

"Are you making any headway on the house?" Grant asked off-handedly.

"I know it's difficult to tell. Everything's a mess," Margaret leaned back in her chair.

Silence.

His gaze scanned the sky, his hands laced behind his head. A thoughtful expression on his face."

"Grant?"

"Yeah?"

"You seem preoccupied. What's wrong?"

"Huh? Just relaxing."

Margaret talked about her plans for the house. He remained silent.

"What do you think?" she repeated. Then she noticed he was sound asleep.

Poor guy must be exhausted Margaret thought. This man warmed her heart and body like no other. She rose from her chair and approached him. Squatting beside him, Margaret placed a kiss on his forehead. With a moan, he gave a faint smile but didn't move.

The air grew cooler by the moment, she couldn't leave him outside to catch a cold. How would she get him upstairs?

"Grant, wake up."

He failed to respond.

"Sweetheart, it's too cold to stay outside." Margaret nudged him. "C'mon." He tossed his head for a moment then rested.

It was a dirty trick, but she couldn't think of another way.

Leaning directly over him, Margaret planted her mouth firmly over his. He responded immediately, releasing a satisfied groan. His arms moved to secure her to him. Grant's mouth began to move under hers. He opened his eyes.

After a long, wet kiss, Margaret withdrew, dizzy. His kiss began at her lips but the tingle went straight to her heart. A familiar warmth filled her abdomen.

"Grant."

"That's a helluva way to wake up," he said huskily, sweeping his lower lip with his tongue.

"I couldn't leave you outside."

"I'm not complaining. You should do it often."

"It was meant to get your attention."

"You have it."

"C'mon, let's get you to bed. You're exhausted," Margaret began.

"I'm tired, but I'm not that tired."

"Forget it. You're going to bed."

"You're right." Slowly he stood.

She helped him upstairs and into bed, tugging his pants off as he lifted his hips. Clad in jockey shorts and tee shirt, Grant leaned back. Margaret covered him with a comforter.

"Join me?" Through heavy lids, he said, "We can keep each other warm."

"Sure, Don Juan." She started for the door. "Sleep well."

~****~

Saturday reared its head this late September day. The weather had traces of autumn, cooler nights with a light breeze. Bleary-eyed, Margaret stretched. The clock radio on her bedside displayed ten o'clock in the morning. She pushed up on elbows and listened. Not a sound was heard. Normally Grant or Hilda would have awakened her by now. But she had been left to slumber. Margaret could hear birds chirping a happy tune outside her window. Everyone chose to sleep in and she wouldn't disturb them. Clad in her gown and robe, Margaret pushed her feet into her slippers and quietly went downstairs. She had worked hard all week, and she deserved coffee in bed.

Stepping into the kitchen, she was greeted by the smell of freshly made coffee. There was a note taped to the coffee maker, she read:

Sorry I had to leave but my daughter's having her baby. I've gone to the hospital. Hilda's visiting her family. Sincerely, Catherine.

Margaret smiled and poured herself a cup. This would hit the spot. Once upstairs, Margaret closed her door and slipped into bed with the hot brew. One of life's simple pleasures was to wake with a good cup of coffee. When she passed Grant's door, she couldn't hear him moving about. He was fatigued she considered.

An hour later Margaret grew weary of the novel she was reading and swung her legs off the bed. She could handle it any longer. The house was uncomfortably quiet. Grant might have left earlier, she would look after a bath.

Forty minutes later she chose to investigate who was up and around. She could hear someone in the kitchen. She followed the sound.

Dressed in only faded jeans, Grant stood by the coffee maker, his back to her. His hair appeared as if he'd slept on top his head. Pouring a cup, he turned slowly. His movements were deliberate, as if in slow motion. He didn't see her at first.

"Good morning, Grant." Her voice almost sang.

"It is, isn't it?" he responded dryly, pushing a hand through his hair and arranging himself on a stool beside the breakfast nook.

"I hope you feel better than you sound," she offered tentatively.

"I'll let you know after I've had two cups of coffee." He lifted the steamy brew to his lips. "Damn, it's hot."

"You're a grouch. And after all that sleep," Margaret teased.

"Okay, Miss Sunshine, save it." Grant scowled.

"Maybe breakfast will improve your disposition?"

"I doubt it. My sinuses give me fits at the change of season. So, can it."

"Yes, sir." She saluted.

He rolled his eyes and lifted the cup to his lips.

Ignoring his ill mood, she plunged ahead taking delight in explaining her progress on the house. As she spoke he responded with an occasional groan. He turned to swing off the stool, his cup in hand. She intervened, taking it from him.

She has a lot of energy he thought. She refilled his cup and handed it to him.

"Still plan to see your parents?"

"Yeah."

"Are you always so gabby in the morning?" Margaret scolded mockingly.

"Margaret you wear me out." He managed a half grin.

"I haven't seen you in three days," she defended.

"Miss me, huh?"

"Whatever gave you that idea?"

"Admit it, you can't live without me." He looked like a Cheshire cat.

"Your ego is definitely to big for your head."

"Yes, dear. I mean, sweetheart." He leaned back on the stool.

"You weren't out-of-it last night. You faker," she accused.

"There's a difference between being out-of-it and being dead," he countered."Sweetheart, I like that." His eyes gleamed mischief.

Margaret blushed. He pushed up from the stool.

Before she realized it, Grant straddled her legs as she sat sideways on the stool and pulled her into his embrace. The kiss was liquid fire.

Instantly he released her.

Spellbound, Margaret said, "Does this mean you're feeling better?"

His eyes danced with merriment. "We've the house to ourselves. What if?"

"Uh," she considered it quickly. "Uh …"

"You said that."

"Do you have an anniversary gift?"

"Stalling, huh?"

"Nope."

He heaved a mock sign of exasperation."Give me thirty minutes, and I'll be ready." He turned to leave, then hesitated."Any ideas?"

"For a gift?" she questioned. He inclined his head. "I'll give it some thought. Go ahead. I'll wait."

He disappeared upstairs.

Most of the afternoon, they browsed the department stores searching for the proper gift. They had a late lunch in Chinatown. Margaret loved the shops in Chinatown, expressing her appreciation of the artwork, beautiful oriental dividers and workmanship – fans, kimonos. Spotting a carved cherry wood hope chest she led Grant over for closer inspection.

"It's old and still in perfect condition," a saleswoman offered, hopefully.

"And expensive," Margaret added. "Although ..." She couldn't relinquish her gaze as she lightly stroked the detailed work with her fingertips.

"We'll take it," Grant said calmly.

"But we don't know the price," Margaret reminded.

"Five thousand dollars," the saleswoman said, as if quoting an insignificant figure.

"Will you accept a check?" he queried.

"Oh yes, sir."

"Can you deliver it?"

"But, Grant --" Margaret blurted.

"Yes, on Monday." The saleswoman smiled pleased with the sale.

"Great." He wrote the check.

"To what address, sir?"

"It's on the check," he replied.

"We'll take care of this first thing Monday," the saleswoman gushed. "Come back and see us."

"Goodbye." Grant guided Margaret from the shop.

"Do you always get what you want despite the cost?"

"Depends how much I want it," he said blandly, then considered the question further. "When I see something I want, I go after it."

"And usually you get it." She finished his sentence. His cocksure attitude irritated Margaret.

"Ordinarily, yes." Grant checked the rearview mirror then drove from the parking lot.

Talk about a silver spoon attitude. Margaret considered Grant had what others only dreamed about money, looks, talent and charm. He was a complete package with arrogance to match. She was incensed.

"Do you want to stop and pick up a card for your parents?"

"I've taken care of that," he remarked casually.

"But, I thought what about the chest?" He didn't appear particularly interested in the piece.

"It's for you."

"What? I can't accept it."

"Why not?"

"It's too expensive."

"I thought you liked it."

"Who wouldn't?"

Grant shot her a sidelong glance. "Then, what's the problem?"

"It's your parents anniversary," she countered, at loss for words.

"My sisters and I have pitched in together for a gift they will love."

"Turn the car around?"

"What?" Grant asked, puzzled.

"To cancel the delivery."

"No."

"Grant I can't let you do this," Margaret said sternly. "You've paid handsomely to redecorate your home."

"I saw the way you admired it."

"You have no right!" she shrieked.

"Just take the damn thing!" he barked. She folded her arms at her waist, seething, but she remained silent. This man would be the death of her.

~****~

Chapter 13

Later that evening, she dressed in a huff, regretting that she agreed to go. The man was incorrigible, spoiled and arrogant. For two cents Margaret would take the next flight back to New York. Once she gave her word she would die before going back on it.

"I don't care what they think of me," Margaret said silently to her reflection, although she checked her appearance several times before leaving the room. The jade crepe de chine dress gave her a regal appearance.

Nervously Grant checked his watch, six o'clock. Alas, she descended the staircase.

Male appreciation filled his eyes, Margaret noticed as she contacted the last step.

She wasn't through being mad at him Margaret reminded herself as he grasp her hand. Bringing it to his lips, Grant placed a kiss on her palm. Stunned, Margaret's anger fled.

"Ready?"

Slowly she nodded.

Thirty minutes later they pulled into the drive of a two-story Tudor home. It was lovely though not as grand as his home. Grant helped her from the car. They walked to the door and knocked. Smiling, Anna opened the door.

"Won't you come in?" Anna gestured with a wave of her hand.

Inside, Grant embraced and kissed his sister.

"I'm glad you could make it," Anna began. She stepped back, shifting her gaze. "Hello, Margaret, I'm Anna."

"Pleased to meet you," Margaret offered demurely.

"Let's go into the living room and sit down," Anna invited.

"Where's mom and dad? Rachael?" Grant questioned.

"Rachael had to work late but she and Chris will arrive at seven. Mom and dad are still dressing.

"I see," Grant replied.

"Would you care for a drink?"

He glanced at Margaret. She shook her head. "We're fine. Thanks." Grant sat next to Margaret on the colonial sofa. His sister took the chair across from them.

Glancing around the room, Margaret said, "Your parents' home is lovely."

"It keeps the rain off our heads," Anna teased.

"Everything ready?" Grant asked, bringing an arm around the back of the sofa.

"Perfect. Mom and dad are as excited as two teenagers," Anna managed. "They're anxious to see you and to meet Margaret."

"How long have your parents been married?" Margaret asked attempting to break the ice. A thousand butterflies danced in her stomach.

"Forty years," he volunteered. "They've lived in the same house from the time they married."

"They were childhood sweethearts," Anna added. "Where did you two meet?"

"St. Raphael's," Margaret responded. "I bumped into your brother in a restaurant."

"Just like that?"

"Not exactly." Margaret glanced at Grant. "Actually, it was later on the beach."

"And it was love at first sight?"

Margaret was relieved when Terrence and Judith Michaels joined them downstairs. Grant shot Anna a I'll-deal-with-you-later look, and Anna appeared oblivious.

"Grant how are you, son?" Judith Michaels greeted as she and her husband stepped into the room. Grant rose and approached them. Judith turned slightly to receive Grant's kiss on her cheek. She hugged him profusely.

"You're a sight for sore eyes." Grant gave Judith a low wolf whistle.

"Now I know why, I've missed having you around," Judith chuckled.

Transferring his gaze to his father, Grant shook Terrence's hand. "How's it going, Dad?"

"Good since you've decided to come home. Your mother has changed clothes let's see." Terrence cupped his chin thoughtfully.

"Don't pay any attention to your father," Judith said, turning. "Are you going to introduce us, son?"

"Mother and dad, I'd like you to meet Margaret Stewart," Grant introduced. "Margaret say hello to Terrence and Judith Michaels, my parents."

"So good of you to come," Judith said, her gaze fixed on Margaret. "Grant's told us so much about you."

"Welcome, Margaret," Terrence added.

"Thank you," Margaret began."Congratulations on your fortieth anniversary."

Judith blushed.

The doorbell rang.

"I'll get it," Anna said as she pushed up from her chair.

Moments later, Anna escorted a tall, dark-haired couple inside. The woman resembled Grant.

"Hello, dear." Judith rose from her chair, embracing the new arrivals. Afterward she supplied, "Rachael and Chris Cooper, please meet Grant's friend, Margaret Stewart. Margaret, Rachael is Grant's older sister, and Chris is Rachael's husband."

"I'm glad to know you," Margaret responded.

"We're pleased to make your acquaintance," Rachael supplied. The Coopers seated themselves on the loveseat across from everyone.

"I think this completes the introductions," Anna murmured. "Thank goodness."

"Mother, shall I ask Nettie to bring in the champagne?" Rachael asked.

Moments later, Rachael returned with a tray of drinks. "Grant would you give me a hand?" Rachael questioned as she approached.

"Sure. What do you want me to do?

"Nettie is tied up with the d'oeuvres."

"Okay." He moved toward the kitchen.

Rachael distributed the champagne then took a seat next to her husband. Shortly, Grant returned with a tray.

"I'd like to propose a toast," Terrence announced, lifting his glass. "Here's to health, happiness and the only woman I have ever loved. Hope she'll put up with me another forty." Laughter filled the room.

"Cheers!" Everyone chimed in.

The Michaels were a closely knit group, warm and caring. Margaret began to feel she belonged after a while.

Judith couldn't wait to speak with Margaret, turning she said, "I understand you're redecorating my son's home?"

"Yes, I am."

"And how's it coming?" Judith remarked pleasantly.

"I've only begun."

"Son, I'd like to show you something," Terrence said, "Margaret will you excuse us?"

"Please don't let me keep you," Margaret responded. Grant shot her a smile and shrugged.

"Judith see to our guests." Terrence turned and left with Grant.

"Margaret is a decorator," Anna informed everyone. "She's from New York."

"The big apple, huh?" Rachael commented after a sip of her drink.

"Girls get acquainted," Chris began. "Think I'll join the men."

This was what Margaret feared most. She would be at the mercy of the women.

"See you later," Rachael called over her shoulder as Chris left the room. "Dinner's at eight."

"Tell us about yourself, Margaret," Judith invited congenially.

"I have a business in New York. I like to think, it's doing well," Margaret evaded.

"What we want to know is, how did you lasso Grant's heart?" Rachael said bluntly.

"That's right just speak your mind, Rachael," Judith scolded.

"Anna said it was love at first sight," Rachael defended.

"Girls!" Judith admonished."You'll have to forgive their tenacity."

"Just exactly what did Grant tell you about me," Margaret asked cautiously.

"It's not what he's said. I've seen the way you look at one another," Anna interjected.

"My son seems taken with you," Judith added. "I'm pleased."

"We're friends," Margaret supplied. Lovers, temporarily she thought.

"Grant's never brought a woman home," Rachael said, prodding."You're a first."

"I think you're making to much of it," Margaret reasoned.

"He's different," Rachael said, puzzled. "He looks content."

"He needs to settle down with a wife and have a family," his mother supplied.

"I think you're under the wrong impression," Margaret explained, exasperated.

"We know Grant better than anyone," Rachael said matter-of-factly. "Frankly I never thought he'd settle for one woman."

"I'm flattered of course."

"Have some champagne," Anna suggested as she noticed Margaret's glass was empty.

This was worse than Margaret had expected. How could Grant have left her to the wolves? "Thank you, I will."

"Don't you care for my son?" Judith queried, concern lacing her voice.

"Yes," Margaret hesitated. She sipped her drink. "He's wonderful."

"Okay ladies, let's retreat shall we?" Grant said crossing the room.

"Just when it was getting interesting," Rachael pouted.

"I should have known better than to leave her to the three of you," Grant chided mockingly."Incidentally, Nettie asked me to announce dinner is served."

Terrence and Chris joined the group as the women rose.

"I hope they didn't give you a bad time," Grant said after everyone left the room.

"No, of course not."

He glanced around the room certain they were alone. Drawing her gently into his arms, Grant gave her a tender kiss. Margaret responded as always, his touch sent pulsing waves throughout her. She moved her arms around his neck. He angled his mouth, and deepened the kiss.

"You have no idea what you do to me," he whispered between kisses.

"Okay, young lovers," Anna teased. "It's time to dine."

Grant ignored the interruption. Margaret withdrew, embarrassed.

"We'll be right in," he supplied.

"Everyone's waiting." Anna turned and departed.

"Lucky for you we're here," Grant managed. "Or I would be making passionate love to you."

"Grant!" Margaret admonished.

"I can't seem to keep my hands off you." His lips took possession of hers once again. Heaving an exasperated sigh, he withdrew. "Ready?"

She bobbed her head.

They entered the dining room.

"I thought we'd have to move dinner into the other room." Anna couldn't resist the temptation.

"My brother misbehaving again?" Rachael questioned.

"Enough, both of you. We have a guest," Terrence reminded.

The meal of red snapper, baked potato, salad and broccoli with cheese sauce was excellent. The anniversary cake was delicious but too sweet for Margaret's taste.

Everyone retreated to the patio to open gifts. Judith opened a large beautifully wrapped box. There were several other gifts waiting for her.

The microwave was a gift from her husband. The printer and computer was a gift from Grant, Anna and Rachael.

Terrence opened a small box addressed to him. Inside was a black onyx ring surrounded by small diamonds, a gift from Judith.

"Read the inscription," Judith coaxed.

Terrence examined the inside of the ring. He read aloud.

"To my one and only hero, Judith. "

"How sweet," Margaret offered.

Tears welled in Terrence's eyes. Judith moved to his side, enfolding him. He kissed her. "Thank you," Terrence said as he withdrew."I might have considered a more personal gift."

"One of the reasons I married you," Judith supplied."Is because you're practical."

"I knew you hated the old one," her husband uttered.

"What made you decide to give your parents a computer and printer?" Margaret asked.

"Mom's been writing for a long time. Every writer should have one. Dad will use the computer, also. He has an idea for a new business."

"Oh, really?"

"Import-export. They want to travel."

"You're right. It's the perfect gift."

Grant turned up the music and persuaded Margaret to join him in dance on the patio. The others went inside to check out the new computer.

"I'm glad you came with me," he whispered in her ear.

"Your family's delightful," she muttered.

"They approve of you."

"How can you tell?"

"They've never teased me like this. Most of the time no one is good enough."

"They want you to be happy."

"How about you?"

"That's a loaded question."

"Maybe."

If his family wanted to fantasize about Grant settling down, this was their misfortune Margaret considered.

She had to get back to reality.

~****~

Chapter 14

Margaret was pleased when Monday arrived, the workers were back on the job. How she managed to hold Grant at bay she would never know. The anniversary party was pleasant, the Michaels were a close loving family. What surprised her most was they tried to marry their son off. They were warm people and they seemed to like her. This was to perfect she reminded herself. Grant was capable of making people believe whatever he wanted them to and accustomed to realizing his desires.

Her work began to take form. She utilized an accent wall in one room and wallpaper in another. Blinds instead of drapes in the smaller rooms made them appear more spacious. She changed the color scheme in a room, added a throw rug in another, and to each room several plants were added. Margaret loved plants. They provided warmth and life to a home.

Noise echoed through the large house. Catherine complained she couldn't think straight. Would the banging ever stop?

Margaret recalled Saturday night when they left Grant's parents. She was politely distant on the return trip. Tonight she was reminded how temporary their relationship was. It was best that she complete the job and return to New York as soon as possible. One thing was to be done, step up the workmen's pace. She had the supplies she needed. She didn't want or need a hopeless relationship.

Margaret recollected the bewildered expression that crossed Grant's face briefly then disappeared. She couldn't be sure. What was it? Hurt or rejection? Suddenly his expression became unreadable. This was too complicated for Margaret. Her life was that of a wild horse in flight with both reins flapping in the breeze. Margaret had to get back on track. She set her coffee cup down and went to work.

~****~

"I'm glad you could join me," Grant said as he gazed across the table to Bill.

"We've known each other fifteen years. Aside from Emily, well," Bill paused. "What's wrong, Grant?"

"I took Margaret to meet the family. I thought it would help," Grant began. "But - "

"But what?"

"She seems more distant that ever."

"And, this troubles you?" Bill tried for a lighter tone.

"I suppose you're right. Who can figure women?"

"If you could, you'd be the first. Women operate off pure emotion. They don't even think like we do," Bill reasoned.

"The problem is," Grant paused.

"You care for her."

"Exactly."

"Have you told her how you feel?"

"No. I've shown her."

"How?"

"We enjoy each other immensely. I bought her an expensive chest she admired. Instead of being appreciative, she was angry. We argued. What's with her?"

"Is there another guy?" Bill questioned.

"There *was* a fiancée, Phillip. But she called it off," he confessed.

"Sounds as though you've met your match. Perhaps the lady likes being single," Bill offered.

"Do you really think so?"

"Consider this, your relationship with her was fine until you moved for a commitment. Then she turned to ice."

Grant considered the idea carefully.

"Women are different nowadays. They're independent, self-sufficient, and are doctors and lawyers or successful business women, like Margaret."

This wasn't what Grant had expected. Bill hadn't helped matters any, he complicated the picture.

"A tease, huh?" Grant's expression grew angry.

"Maybe. Or perhaps she likes your body," Bill entertained. "What's wrong with that?"

No response.

"I have to get back," Grant hedged. "Thanks."

"I hope it helped."

~****~

The doorbell rang just as Margaret passed. She opened the door.

"Michaels residence?" a burly man inquired.

"Yes, it is."

"I have a delivery. Sign here, please." The man pushed a clipboard into her hands.

She reached out for the clipboard. "What is it?"

"How should I know lady? I just deliver them." The man turned on his heel and returned moments later with a large box mounted on a dolly."Where do you want it?"

Margaret read the label: *The Yum Yum Tree*. She forgot about the hope chest, and she released a deep sigh. "Upstairs."

"You're kidding?"

"I wish I were."

"Oh, lady!" He studied her in disbelief. "It's gonna be one of those days." He started toward the stairs.

A worker assisted the delivery man. Minutes later the cherry wood chest gleamed in the sunlight that gently bathed the room. Margaret sat on the bedside staring at it. One problem after another she considered.

That night and the next few Grant didn't come home until the wee hours. He had almost become a phantom Margaret thought.

On Thursday, Hilda informed Margaret that Grant would be away for a week, maybe two. They were filming on location. Hilda would pack his bag and send it to the studio. He would leave from there.

How inconsiderate Margaret mused. Great, he wouldn't be underfoot. Evidently he realized his mistake and was gracefully bowing out.

Each day passed slowly for Margaret. Although she worked twelve hour days, it didn't help. The workers complained but she was relentless. Grant's home would be a showcase, warm and inviting, restful yet reflect the man. This would be her best work.

Catherine tried to make excuses for her boss but Margaret wasn't buying it. He's a master of relationships.

A week passed without a call or note from Grant. She became moody, and this was uncharacteristic of Margaret. The man upset the balance in her life.

The renovation came together better than she'd ever hoped. It was truly a masterpiece.

Wednesday morning brought a telephone call Margaret had not considered.

Where was Hilda or Catherine? When the telephone continued to ring, Margaret greeted,

"Hello, Michaels residence?"

"Margaret?" a female voice greeted over the wire.

"Yes?"

"It's Anna. How are you?"

"Oh, Anna. I'm fine. I'm trying to finish up. You should see the house." Margaret's voice was laced with pride.

"I'd like to."

"Come on over," Margaret suggested.

"See you in an hour." Anna rang off. The house had become lonely without Grant. The servants tried to care for her. But it wasn't the same. She missed New York, her parents and Popcorn. Her poor cat probably thought she deserted him.

"Miss Stewart, what about the cabinet?" the carpenter queried.

"No, that will not do. We will need the larger one."

"Yes, ma'am."

It was ten o'clock and Anna was due to arrive in thirty minutes. She would change clothes.

"Margaret I love it," Anna gushed."This doesn't look like the same place. Grant will be pleased."

"I hope so."

"He hasn't seen it?"

"He's away on location."

"No wonder, I haven't heard from him. Where?"

"He didn't tell me," Margaret admitted.

"Surely he's called?" Anna sensed trouble. I haven't heard from Grant since the anniversary party."

Hilda met the women in the foyer. "Will Ms. Anna join you for lunch?"

Margaret's gaze held Anna's. She waited.

"If that's an invitation, I accept," Anna interjected.

"We'll eat on the patio. It's one of the quieter spots," Margaret said casually.

Hilda nodded her approval and departed. Margaret noticed the frown on Anna's face, as they started for the patio.

"Margaret is there trouble between you and Grant?"

A flush covered Margaret's face.

"Tell me about it?"

"I'm not sure I should," she hedged.

"Did you and Grant quarrel?"

No response followed.

"I'd like to help if I can," Anna coaxed.

"You're in love," Anna commented matter-of-factly.

"Yes, but," Margaret confessed. "He --"

"He's crazy about you," Anna blurted. "You've had him in a tail spin from the start."

"I know about his reputation with women. He's unaccustomed to hearing no." Margaret pleated her napkin on the table. "I present a temporary challenge."

"And you think it's no basis for a lasting relationship?"

"Exactly. And there's another problem."

"If you love one another, all problems can be overcome."

"His life is in California, whereas mine is in New York. Long distance romances never work."

"You miss him?"

"Terribly."

"My guess is, he's just as miserable. Grant and I have always been close."

"He's arrogant and we argue over nothing."

"Grant's spoiled. As far as he'd concerned, this is unfamiliar turf. He always retreats when he needs time to think."

"You really think so?"

"I'd be willing to bet on it. He loves you but if you tell him I said so, I'll deny it."

Margaret's heavy heart lightened with renewed hope. Since the usual methods failed, he's trying to figure out how he'll deal with the situation." Anna laughed.

"It never hurts to learn humility."

She carried the disappointment long enough, it felt good to admit her feelings Margaret thought.

"What would you suggest?"

"Let him make the next move. You've got him right where you want him."

Both laughed.

"Okay," Margaret beamed.

Anna rose.

"Won't you stay for lunch?"

"No. I have an idea." Anna winked and turned to take her leave. "See you later."

~****~

Later that night, Margaret picked up the novel she had begun, just as the telephone rang. She glanced at the clock radio. It was ten o'clock. Grant? she thought.

Anxiously she grabbed the phone.

"Hello?" a voice greeted. "Margaret?"

"Yes, momma. How are you?"

Elisia burst into tears.

"What's wrong?"

"Your father's had a heart attack. He's in intensive care."

"Mother, take it easy. I'll leave first thing in the morning," Margaret reassured. After a short conversation, Elisia hung up.

Margaret called to schedule her flight to New York. She disliked leaving on short notice but it couldn't be helped. She had no idea of Grant's whereabouts. Her immediate concern was her father.

Much later and exhausted, she fell asleep.

Early the next morning, Margaret informed Catherine and Hilda that her father had taken ill. After writing a note to Grant, she asked the chauffeur to drive her to the airport.

Anxiously, Margaret waited for her flight to be announced. Life was short. She was so busy with her own life, she had neglected her parents. They'd always been there for her, encouraging her. She vowed things would change.

Please Lord, don't let him die!

Margaret felt numb inside.

On arrival in New York, the 747 glided smoothly to a stop on the runway. She took a taxi to the hospital. The elevator to the fourth floor seemed longer than the entire trip. Didn't these people understand her father's life hung in the balance? People who boarded and departed the elevator took forever she thought. Margaret bit her lower lip as one person held the elevator for a friend. The elevator digital read: Four. At last! She pushed through the crowd.

Approaching the nurse's station, Margaret located her mother. Elisia looked pale and this frightened her. She embraced her mother. Each clutched the other like a life line.

"How is he?"

"The doctor said the next 48 hours will tell the story," Elisia murmured. "He's resting."

"C'mon, you should eat something," Margaret encouraged.

"What if something happens?"

"If you don't take care of yourself, you won't be much good to him."

Elisia bobbed her head.

"Wait here." Margaret approached a nurse who was busily writing in a patient's chart.

"May I help you?" the nurse asked pleasantly.

"Yes. I'm Mr. Stewart's daughter. My mother and I will be in the cafeteria if you need us."

"Alright. I will notify his nurse."

"Thank you."

Downstairs Elisia led the way to the cafeteria. Margaret couldn't remember when she had seen her mother so vulnerable.

"He's so weak. They have him hooked to a lot of wires. An EKG to monitor his heart," Elisia sniffled. "And he has an I.V."

"When can we see him?" Margaret queried.

"The nurse just bathed him. She asked me to wait an hour."

"Let's have something to eat then see him," Margaret suggested, attempting control. Inside she trembled with fear.

Please don't let him die! she cried silently. You don't want him, Lord.

Elisia followed mechanically, relieved to have her daughter near. Once seated with their trays, Margaret began talk about her assignment as a diversion. She had been in California five weeks.

"Another week or so, I should finish the job. And mother, you should see it. I'll take some pictures."

"You've always had an eye for color and balance," Elisia managed. "How did Grant Michaels take your sudden departure?"

"He's away on location. I left him a message."

"I see," Elisia said blandly. Her thoughts shifted to her husband.

Margaret patted her mother's hand reassuringly. He's going to make it. You'll see. He's too stubborn to die."

Elisia smiled faintly.

"Now finish your coffee."

Moments later they rode the elevator to the fourth floor and stepped out.

"May we see Mr. Stewart?" Margaret asked a nurse at the desk.

Another nurse walked out of her father's room and smiled. She repeated the question. They were instructed to visit fifteen minutes and not to excite him. He was asking for them.

"Thank you," Margaret called over her shoulder as both women started for his room.

"Hello, daddy," Margaret said, kissing his forehead.

"Hello, kitten," Brian Stewart said softly."Your mother shouldn't have worried you."

"Never mind that. How's the food?" she replied casually.

"Lousy. " Brian made an attempt at humor.

"How do you feel?"

"I've felt better. This sure scared the hell out of me," Brian admitted. His wife squeezed his hand.

"I know, daddy. Anything we can bring you?"

"Yeah. Some pajamas. The damn things don't cover a man's pride," Brian said, grabbing his gown with one hand. He laughed softly. His eyelids fluttered to his cheek.

"I'll take care of it." Margaret leaned to kiss him. "We'll see you later. I love you."

He nodded as he drifted to sleep.

Elisia looked as though she might pass out from exhaustion at any moment. Both women walked out of the room. Mr. Stewart's nurse approached.

"The doctor was here earlier. He said Mr. Stewart's lab work has improved. He's out of danger. We're keeping him in ICU another day for observation then he'll go out to the floors. He's a lucky man."

"Thank you," Margaret said, relieved.

"Incidentally take Mrs. Stewart home. We'll call if there's any change in his condition," the nurse added. Both women glanced toward his room. "I'll tell him."

After claiming her bag from the information attendant, Margaret hailed a cab.

"Thank God," Elisia said after they boarded the taxi.

"I know mother."

Forty-five minutes later, the taxi dropped them at the Stewart residence. Margaret made sure her mother took a hot bath and went to bed.

An hour later, Margaret sank into a chair. Her mother fell asleep the moment her head hit the pillow. A sigh of relief escaped Margaret.

"Meow?"

"Oh baby, I'm glad to see you," Margaret cried, hugging Popcorn. A steady stream of tears followed. The cat sensed her pain and remained nearby until both fell asleep.

~****~

**Chapter 15**

"Anyone home?" Grant called as he walked through the silent house.

No response followed.

He flipped on lights as he moved through the house. He found a note in the kitchen and read:

Mr. Michaels,

My daughter needs me to babysit this weekend. It's Hilda's weekend off. I almost forgot, there's a message from Miss Stewart on your desk in the study.

Catherine

Grant opened the refrigerator and threw a sandwich together. It was nine o'clock and he was starved. Taking a large bite of the chicken salad sandwich, he ambled into the study. He opened the envelope and read:

Grant,

My father's had a heart attack. I've gone to New York to be with him. I'm not sure when I will return. Margaret

He grabbed a bottle of Perrier from the small fridge, taking a large swallow. It served him right he thought as he took another bite of the sandwich. He'd left without a word. But he needed time alone, to think. Margaret turned him inside out. Two weeks away confirmed his fears. He loved her desperately. He didn't know how he would tell her, but he would.

In addition, he was concerned with other matters. Grant was unhappy with his lifestyle for some time. But habits were hard to break. It took courage to strike out in a new direction. He vowed he would quit after this movie. It was time for a complete change. He had always enjoyed writing. Grant hoped Margaret would be waiting for him. Lifting the receiver he punched the number for information.

"For what city?" a gravelly voice greeted.

"New York City."

"Name, please?"

He didn't know her father's name. Damn! "Never mind." Grant hadn't bothered to learn more about her. He couldn't believe his ineptitude Perhaps it was best. "Thank you." Grant replaced the receiver. He tried Margaret's number. It rang and rang. "Damn it!" If only she'd turned on her machine. She didn't expect him to call a small voice within him scolded.

~****~

Margaret woke at nine the next morning. Still her mother's door remained closed. She pushed up to an upright position in bed and reached for the telephone book.

"ICU, please."

"ICU, Miss Foreman. May I help you?"

"Yes. May I speak to Brian Stewart's nurse? This is his daughter."

"Mr. Stewart is doing well. He had a good night. In fact, he's sassy," the nurse chuckled.

"That sounds like my father."

"We're transferring him to the medical-surgical floor, room 543 in one hour."

"Thank you, Miss Foreman."

Margaret was elated she could almost dance a jig. Moments later she prepared coffee as she hummed to herself. Popcorn arched his back and rubbed against her leg.

"It's a happy day, Popcorn!" Margaret said as she washed his bowls and filled one with water. Popcorn's tail rose quivering in the air as she opened the can of cat food with the electric can opener.

"Good morning, dear," Elisia said as she stepped into the kitchen. "I take it, you've already called the hospital?"

"Yes. Dad's giving the nurses a bad time. Isn't that wonderful?" Margaret managed. "They plan to transfer him to the fifth floor, room 543."

"Thank heaven," Elisia commented "I'll have a cup too. This ordeal has taken years off my life." Margaret set the coffee mugs on the table and lowered herself into a chair.

Elisia and Margaret visited Brian Stewart at twelve noon.

"It's good to see you with color in your face," Elisia said approvingly.

~****~

Two days later, Brian Stewart was released with strict instructions to rest.

"I have some marketing to do," Elisia sighed. "Make sure your father behaves, Margaret."

"He'll be fine."

Elisia turned and closed the door behind her.

"It's your move, kitten," Brian remarked after his play. The two always enjoyed a good game of checkers.

"What?"

"I said, it's your move," Brian repeated. "You don't have your mind on the game."

"I'm sorry. Let's see." She studied the possibilities and made her move.

Immediately Brian jumped two of Margaret's men, picking them up. "It's no fun if it's too easy."

No response followed.

"What's wrong, kitten?"

"Nothing," she sighed.

"This is your dad, remember?"

"You could always see through me."

"Want to tell me about it?" Brian began. "Man trouble?"

"How did you know?"

"Just a shot in the dark. Let's say I recognize the signs. You love him?"

"Yes, but …"

"Is he in love with you?"

"I don't know."

"Either he does or does not. Which is it?"

"He makes me feel alive, whole and important when I'm with him."

"How does he react toward you?"

"The same way. We enjoy each other for awhile, then everything explodes. We argue, and I'm confused."

"You met him in California?"

"No, St. Raphael's. His name is Grant Michaels, he's an actor."

"I see," Brian said thoughtfully."The man's well known and prominent."

"You forgot, arrogant as well. He thinks he owns me."

"It appears he holds the key to your heart."

"There's more to a relationship than a physical attraction. Loyalty, respect and consideration for one another are important. You don't demand them, you earn them."

"Has he mistreated you?"

"No. He expects me to be at his beckon call, not to question him."

"Kitten, a man is raised to be strong, to defend his home and to protect what's his and to be a good provider. Sometimes it's difficult for him to express himself, to be vulnerable. He fears rejection.We all do," Brian explained.

"When you dated mom, were you bossy and arrogant?" Margaret queried.

"No. Some people find it more difficult than others to express themselves. Strong willed, independent people like yourself," Brian reminded."Have you told him how you feel?"

She shook her head.

"You refuse to make the first move? Pride can keep people from loving you dearly," Brian explained."Some people live a lifetime and never experience true love. Don't throw it away because of pride."

"I'll think it over, daddy."

"Grant's a man with a large ego. He's handsome. It goes with the territory. Think about it."

"Thanks, daddy. I will." Margaret kissed his cheek and crossed the room to the door.

Brian smiled to himself as he turned to his side to rest.

Could Grant be as fearful of commitment as she? Everyone seemed to think he loved her. Margaret wanted to believe it. She lifted the receiver and punched out his number.

Please let him be home!

It was Tuesday night, Grant arrived four days ago. He glanced at the clock, ten o'clock. There hadn't been a call or letter from Margaret. Although Catherine and Hilda were loyal, they admitted to Grant that he ran Margaret off with his cool attitude. He didn't blame her.

Grant propped both feet on the sofa in the study. Jazz bellowed from the compact disc player. He knew he'd blown it, but good. The scotch began to ease his aching heart.

The telephone rang. If the music hadn't been so loud, Grant might have heard it. It continued to ring.

Anna lifted the receiver. "Hello?"

"What are you doing there, Anna?" Margaret blurted..

"Well, hello to you, too."

"I'm sorry. Is Grant there?"

"I've been with him since Sunday when I found him drunk. Someone has to look out for him!" Irritation filled Anna's voice.

"When did he return?"

"Friday. Where are you?"

"New York."

"Is he alright?"

"Grant's trying to douse his pain with drink," Anna said brusquely. "Don't bother coming back, unless you're serious about him."

"I didn't run out on him. He's the one who left without a word," Margaret retorted. "When I couldn't reach him, I left a message. My father's had a heart attack."

"I'm sorry, Margaret. I didn't know," Anna apologized. "How is your father faring?"

"We brought him home today. Didn't Catherine or Hilda mention I left for New York?"

"Catherine's daughter went out of the country with her husband on business. I told Hilda I would stay with Grant for awhile. He's a real mess. He won't shave or anything. He needs you, Margaret."

"I'll leave in the morning," Margaret reassured. "Stay with him until I arrive, will you?"

"Of course." Anna hung up.

Anna heard music and moved toward the study. Grant was asleep on the sofa. An empty glass rested on a nearby table. A beard shadowed his jaw. Anna turned off the compact disc player and covered him. She would be glad to see Margaret. The man was destroying himself.

Margaret began to pack her bag. She called the airlines for a reservation, then walked into the living room.

"It's good to have you home again," Elisia said as her daughter sat across from her on the sofa.

"Thanks mom," Margaret began. "Since dad's alright, I need to return to California. I've a job to finish."

"You called him?" Elisia continued to knit.

"So daddy told you?"

Elisia nodded.

"He needs me mother," she explained."And I need him. I love him."

"That's a start. At least you admit it."

"You understand?"

"Absolutely. You have our blessings and our love."

"Thank you, mother." Margaret embraced her.

The following day, Brian teased, "Invite us to the wedding."

"You'll be the first to know. Thanks for everything."

"Can I drive you to the airport?" Elisia asked.

"I'll take a cab. Dad needs you here," Margaret said as she gathered her carry-on bag.

~****~

The flight to Los Angeles seemed to take forever Margaret reflected.

"Care for a glass of complimentary champagne?" the stewardess asked.

"No, thank you. But I will have a strawberry daiquiri," Margaret responded.

What would she say to him? Would Grant be pleased to see her or cross?

The plane made three stops along the way with two hour layover in Dallas. She tried to telephone Grant, but there was no answer.

"Ladies and gentlemen, please fasten your seat belts and extinguish your cigarettes. We are approaching Los Angeles

International Airport. It's 75 degrees. Enjoy your stay," the stewardess announced.

A glimpse of her watch displayed seven o'clock. The 747 landed effortlessly. Margaret stepped from the plane and managed to push her way through the crowd. Outside she boarded a taxi.

"Where to lady?" the driver asked.

She gave him instructions and leaned back in the seat with a sigh. Wednesday night traffic was heavy. Red lights flashed ahead.

"Looks like a wreck up ahead," the driver informed.

What else, she thought. Why was it the last few steps of a journey seemed to take the longest her heart cried.

An hour later traffic cleared and they were on their way once more. Margaret arrived at eight-thirty. She rang the doorbell.

"Grant, get that will you?" Anna shouted from the kitchen.

"No problem." He sauntered to the door and swung it open. His smile changed to a frown.

"Hello, Grant. How are you?"

"Margaret, what?" He hesitated. "Come in." She entered.

"Here let me take that." Grant took her carry-on bag.

Anna moved into the foyer. "Welcome back, Margaret." They embraced.

What's wrong with Anna? She's a traitor he considered.

"Thank you," Margaret acknowledged.

"Hungry?"Anna asked with enthusiasm.

"Starving."

"I've made dinner." Anna turned to Grant. "I meant to tell you, Rachael called. Her babysitter called off at the last minute and she needs me to babysit."

~****~

**Chapter 16**

"Go ahead," Grant replied."Thanks for everything." He kissed Anna's cheek. "Caleb will drive you."

"Sorry I must run, Margaret. See you later." With her back to her brother, Anna winked.

Grant pushed a button on the intercom and called for the car.

"I'll wait outside." Anna opened the door and walked out.

They stared at one another for an extended moment.

"Forgive me. I'm sure you're fatigued," Grant began. "Shall we?" He gestured toward the dining room.

Candlelight, soft music and a formally set table for two awaited them.

"It seems Anna's thought of everything," Grant commented."Welcome back." He pulled back her chair as she lowered herself.

"It's good to be here."

He arranged himself in a chair across from her. "How's your father?"

"He will be fine with the proper diet and rest." Margaret flashed what she hoped was her best smile.

"That's good news." A broad smile covered his face. "Care for some white wine?"

"Please."

He poured a glass for each of them. After sipping his wine, he said, "I tried to phone several times while you were in New York. But I didn't know your parents name."

"Brian and Elisia Stewart."

"I didn't think you'd come back."

"Why?" Margaret prodded.

"Well …" Grant faltered. "The way I've treated you. Guess I wouldn't blame you."

"Why did you leave without a word?" she uttered as her index finger traced the top of her glass.

"I'd like to apologize," he hedged."I needed time alone."

Throwing caution to the wind, she smiled."Why?"

"I care a great deal for you, Margaret. You must know that. The mixed signals you sent, confused me."

"Have you found the answer?"

"I've had time to sort things out," he replied calmly.

"And?"

"I don't want to be without you."

"Long distance romances never work."

"That's what I want to talk to you about," Grant added.

"What do you hope to accomplish?" she asked with a broad smile.

"We'll talk after dinner."

They lingered over dinner. The meal of stuffed flounder, scalloped potatoes, salad and rice was delectable.

Soft jazz filled the room.

"Dance with me?" he urged.

She rose and moved into his arms. He drew her closer than necessary barely moving to the music.

It felt like the fourth of July to Margaret, her pulse drummed in her ears and her stomach fluttered.

Grant slid a hand to her low back, then moved the other to draw her across his arm. He rained kisses along the hollow of her neck, and moved with quiet desperation to her lips.

A sigh of satisfaction escaped Grant. "Margaret, I've been a fool. Don't ever –" His mouth crashed down on hers. After an extended moment he continued, "leave me, again."

"I've missed you terribly," she confessed.

Grant lost control. He wanted and needed her.

He fumbled with the buttons on her blouse. Frustrated after several attempts, he tore it open.

"Grant, please," she whimpered. "Someone might see us."

"We're alone," he explained in a whisper. "I need you, baby. You drive me crazy."

Margaret reveled that she affected him this way.

"Let's go for a swim?" She stepped onto the patio. Slipping out of her clothes, she dove into the pool. Grant followed close behind.

Feverishly he scrambled out his clothes and entered the water. He was beside her in seconds, turning her into his embrace. Her legs encircled his waist. His mouth covered a pouting nipple. A soft cry escaped her lips as Margaret's hands applied light pressure to the back of his head.

"Do you like that?" he whispered.

"Yes. Oh, yes."

"Tell me, Margaret. I need to hear," he coaxed.

"I've missed you," she evaded.

"You know what I want to hear," Grant said, lifting his head, his eyes dark with desire. "Tell me, now." He took a rosy bud in his mouth and cupped her bottom.

Margaret's senses exploded with need. She moved against him. "Grant, I love you. Take me, now."

He paused for a moment, then thrust fast and purposefully into her. "Tell me, how do you feel?" he urged.

"Wonderful. I've wanted you so," she confessed.

"Oh, you feel so good," he moaned. His thrusts increased in depth and frequency, launching them into an abyss. "Hold me. Oh, yes." Collapsing against her, he kissed her tenderly.

She clung to him helplessly. She would take him on any terms. He made her feel whole. She loved him mindlessly.

A gentle breeze began to blow. Margaret trembled.

"C'mon love, let's go inside," he murmured. She bobbed her head.

Did he mean it the way it sounded? Or were his words spoken in the heat of passion?

He drew her along his length before lifting her easily onto the edge of the pool. Grant levered himself out of the water. His body was magnificent, Margaret thought.

Turning Margaret scurried inside giggling as he chased her upstairs. She stumbled at the top of the stairs. He lifted her effortlessly into his arms, entered his bedroom, then kicked the door shut. Gently he lowered her on the king size bed. Her eyes mirrored the desire that held him. He was hard, again. As he edged his knee between her thighs, Grant lightly pushed her back on the bed. Her hands stroked his chest at first, lingering at his nipples, then moved slowly to his groin. A low guttural moan escaped him.

"Do you like that?" she asked huskily.

"You know I do, temptress." He took a deep breath.

"How much?" Margaret taunted. She would make him admit his feelings.

"Enough to ask, you to do it again."

She moved provocatively against him."What do you want?"

"You, in my bed always," he admitted, writhing against her.

Margaret knew she should be horse whipped, but she couldn't resist the temptation."Why?"

She pushed him onto his back. Grant shook his head.

"Because," he moaned.

"Tell me why?" she persisted.

"I need you," he offered.

She shook her head. Leaning over him, she brushed the tips of her breasts against his cheek. "Say the magic word."

He heaved a deep sigh, lifting his head, he grabbed her. His possession was complete in one swift movement, he lay sprawled along her length. Their coupling hit him like molten, exploding lava. "Because," he kissed her neck and shoulders. "I love you."

"That's all, I wanted to hear," Margaret whispered in his ear. They made love all night then fell asleep, their bodies intertwined.

~****~

The telephone woke them the next morning.

"Hello?" Grant said sleepily.

"How are you, little brother?"

"What do you want, Anna?"

"I'm downstairs. Looks like a real mess here with dishes on the tables, clothes by the pool," Anna prodded. "It must've been some party."

"Okay, okay." He hung up the phone.

"What's wrong?"

"Anna's downstairs. She knows."

Margaret pushed up on her elbows in bed.

"Don't be in a rush," Grant scolded.

"Please, Grant." Margaret covered herself with a sheet.

"What are we to do?" he asked calmly.

"What do *you* suggest?" Margaret countered.

"I think you should move to California."

Her eyes were unreadable. Grant took a deep breath.

"I want you in my life." He kissed the nape of her neck. "Need you in my life."

"Stay here?"

Grinning, he nodded.

"I wouldn't enjoy being your mistress." She shook her head most assuredly.

"You're trying my patience," Grant warned. "What else do you want?"

"The brass ring," she retorted.

He swallowed hard. "Marriage?"

"The whole ball of wax. I'm worth it, " she managed. "You said you loved me."

"I do. But that's blackmail," he shot back.

"If that's the way you see it?" Slowly shaking her head, Margaret swung her legs off the bed.

With her blonde hair cascading to her waist, she had a well-loved look he thought as she padded toward the bathroom. His voice cracked, "You win."

She stopped dead in her tracks. He moved to her side, drawing her into his arms.

"I love you, Margaret. I want you to be my wife." Grant's gaze locked with hers.

"Do you mean it?"

"With all my heart," he responded. "Will you marry me?"

"I thought you'd never ask."

Hurriedly they showered and dressed because Anna was downstairs waiting.

Anna had cleared the mess by the time they joined her. "Ah, the love birds decided to get up," Anna teased.

Margaret blushed.

"As if you didn't know," Grant said calmly. "You set this up."

Anna giggled. "I see it worked."

"Margaret has agreed to marry me," Grant announced proudly.

"It's about time. I love you little brother but, you needed a shove. Mom and dad will be thrilled. So, when is the happy day?"

"Immediately," he supplied.

"What about the house?" Margaret asked sheepishly.

"It can wait. We can't." He lowered his forehead to rest upon hers.

"It takes time to plan a wedding," she countered.

"Nope."

"No?"

"We can be married by the ship's captain," Grant added.

"I like a man who knows what he wants." Margaret laughed.

Anna slipped quietly out the door. It was clear, she was no longer needed.

~****~

**Epilogue**

"But we didn't bring any clothes or -- " Margaret reasoned.

"For once Margaret be spontaneous. The ship leaves in twenty minutes."

"I don't have a wedding dress or …"

"I'll buy you one on board."

"You won't tell anyone?" Margaret whispered in his ear.

"You little hypocrite." He chuckled.

"Where are we going on our honeymoon?"

"It's a surprise."

They were married on the large vessel by the ship's captain just as Grant promised. The ceremony was simple but beautiful. Two anxious onlookers served as witnesses.

"Do you take this man for your lawfully wedded husband, Margaret Elisia Stewart?" the captain asked.

"I do."

And do you take this woman for your lawfully wedded wife, Grant Michaels?" the captain asked. Grant's eyes were fixed on the woman he loved.

"I do."

Simultaneously they said, "For richer or poorer, in sickness or in health. Till death, doeth part."

"I pronounce you man and wife. You may kiss the bride," the captain instructed.

Grant took her in his arms and kissed her thoroughly. A crowd had accumulated on board by now. Cheers of congratulations followed.

"Well, Mrs. Michaels, let's make a run for it." Grant clasped her hand as the crowd began to move in. He guided her to their room.

Just outside their cabin, Margaret exclaimed, "Wait!"

"Why?"

"Haven't you forgotten something?"

"You're right. I forgot to pay the captain." He laughed at her dismay. Lifting her into his arms, he carried her across the threshold and kicked the door shut. Grant tossed her lightly on the bed and turned.

"Did you forget something else?"

"Yes." He held up a *do not disturb* sign and wriggled his eyebrows. "This should ensure our privacy until we reach our destination."

"I bet." She leaned back with a smile.

He hung the sign outside the door.

Three days later, the sign remained on the door. At intervals a porter delivered food and carried away the trays that accumulated outside the door.

"Where are we going for the honeymoon?" Margaret asked again for the umpteenth time.

"It depends on how well I can walk," Grant said mockingly.

"Bragging or complaining?"

"Bragging. My parents wondered how long they'd have to wait before I married and supplied them with a grandson," Grant began. "They may not have long to wait."

"You could be right." Margaret heard a commotion outside on deck. "Sounds as if we've reached land."

A knock sounded at the door.

"Sir, we've reached St. Raphael's."

"Thank you," Grant replied.

"So that's the surprise!" Margaret threw herself into his arms. "Oh Grant, you're so sentimental."

"I wanted to take you back to where I first fell in love with you," he responded softly. "That first night in the restaurant."

"Oh, Grant."

This was truly paradise Margaret thought.

~ THE END ~

ABOUT THE AUTHOR

Melisant Scott is an aficionada of the romance genre. She has enjoyed reading romance novels for several years, alas she decided to try her hand at writing. She hopes everyone enjoys reading, *Paradise Caribbean Style*, a love story about a runaway bride, who literally collides with her male counterpart, sparks ignite and love blossoms. Melisant's hobbies include sailing, music, classic movies, her cats and her home is Texas.

Other books by Melisant Scott are *A Matter Of Convenience* and *Reluctant Heart*. To purchase your copy of Melisant Scott's books on the internet visit: *Open Window Publications*. Most of her romance books are available in both paperback and digital (e-books) formats. Be sure to follow Melisant Scott on *Facebook* or *Twitter*. Watch for the release of her next book, *Forbidden Passion*.

Resources: facebook.com/scottmelisant ; twitter.com/melisantscott ; openwindowpublications.com ; melisantscott.org ; amazon.com/author/MelisantScott

www.ingramcontent.com/pod-product-compliance
Lightning Source LLC
Chambersburg PA
CBHW071150260626
47162CB00003B/986